I0662436

OPERATION
BLACK SWAN

RICHARD LE NORMAND

Le Normand, Richard
Operation Black Swan
ISBN-13: 978-0-9750000-1-4
pp230

Also by Richard le Normand:
A Killer at Large
Escape to Death
Play the Last Card

To my dear sister Ruth Elston,
who gave me so much support before her death in 2012

ABOUT THE AUTHOR

Richard Le Normand was born in Jersey Channel Islands in 1927 and was educated at Victoria College Jersey 1936–1944. Richard left college early, to avoid being 'press-ganged' into the construction of German fortifications—most of the 'slave workers' having been killed off by then and labour was needed to complete their fortifications in Alderney, a sister isle.

After the Islands were liberated in 1945, Richard became a farmer, later specialising in intensive flower and tomato growing under glass. Richard then established a plastics factory to develop and produce new inventions, mainly in the horticultural field.

In 1987, Richard decided to retire and settle in Australia. He soon realised that retirement was not for him and became involved in marketing hydroponics. After spending nine interesting years working in real estate, Richard moved to the Gold Coast where he developed and patented an attachment for small boats. Finally, to pay for all his past sins, Richard started to write and publish books and short stories.

Richard recently released a self-published novel, *A Killer at Large*—the story that precedes and sets the scene for *Escape to Death*. The so-far unpublished novel, *Play the Last Card*, concludes this tale, following the journey of Marcel as a teenager, through to the young man coping with the vicissitudes and indeed, horrors of war. As promised, Richard Le Normand is now offering these three novels as a trilogy.

Additionally, Richard has contributed three very different short stories about the random moments when we mortals lose control of time, to the anthology, *A Leap in Time*, a new literary work just published by the Carindale Writers Group. The anthology writers are all Queensland writers and the stories include fiction, non-fiction and poetry.

CHAPTER 1

In a basement room at the War Office in Canberra, an old overhead fan creaked and grunted, struggling to keep the room cool. It was March 1942, and the Australian summer was drawing to a close.

Major James Bennington and Sergeant Anthony Symons sat silently staring at each other across the major's desk. Outside of their office they could hear the noisy commotion: intelligence had just confirmed that the Japanese Imperial forces had been preparing and were now ready to launch an invasion of Australia. The unthinkable had happened; Australia was on the brink of an invasion by Japan.

The major was a dapper thirty-five year old. He had a couple of deep-set scars on his face from a mission in North Africa when he'd succeeded in pulling out two of his crew members from a burning tank. So now for his reward, he was stuck with this desk job.

Sergeant Symons, ten years his junior, was fresh faced and eager for action. After having successfully completed his training, his ability and strong character were quickly noted by his commanding officer and he was soon promoted to the rank of sergeant. He had been sent on to headquarters to be held ready for any special tasks that might evolve.

1

For the last half hour, they had been mulling over the instructions they had just received from the major's superior, Brigadier Nollybenn, who had returned from an important but sombre War Council meeting that morning.

'I have just come from the War Council meeting. As you must have already heard, it is considered most likely that Japan will attempt to invade Australia. Because of our present depleted forces, it is now highly possible that large parts of northern Australia could be occupied by Japan.

'In view of this serious situation, the council has decided to establish a number of secret arms caches, which will be available for use by a large underground resistance movement operating in some parts of occupied Australia.' He placed a thick brown envelope on the major's desk.

'You two men have been chosen to establish a secret arms cache somewhere on the Myall Lakes, which is north of Port Stephens in New South Wales.'

What the brigadier did not tell them about was the involvement of the treasury. A large amount of gold bullion was to be included with the arms, to be hidden from the invading Japanese and used to fund future operations against the Japanese forces.

'We are now in a very serious situation with diminished forces and very little time for preparation of these arms caches. You will buy and prepare a fishing boat that will carry all your gear and building materials and you will then sail the boat up to the Myall Lakes.' The brigadier lowered his voice. 'We have been told to treat this operation with utmost urgency; and of course you must realise it has been classified as top secret. The fishing boat will be your cover and will be accepted by the locals.'

★

News was not good. On February 19th, just days after the fall of Singapore, Darwin was heavily bombed by the Japanese air force, several ships were sunk and others were badly damaged with considerable loss of life. A whole squadron of RAAF fighter aircraft was destroyed, both in the air and on the ground.

Broome suffered the same fate on March 3rd, with many aircraft, including sixteen flying boats, destroyed. Also, a great number of men, women and children had escaped from Java only to be killed or injured in Australia.

Brigadier Nollybenn looked grave and continued: 'Vast areas of Northern Australia are undefended and with the Allied naval forces now depleted, it would be easy for the Japanese to invade our country. Intelligence reports that invasion plans by Japan are already in place. Of course, we now have the Americans here to help us and although their numbers are at present limited, many more will eventually arrive in Australia. But in the meantime, what you have been ordered to do might become a necessary last resort. Your mission is just part of a large network of last ditch defences now underway.

'If we are overrun by the Japanese,' the brigadier went on, 'a resistance force will have the arms to fight back until the Japs are finally driven out of Australia.'

The brigadier picked up the envelope and handed it to the major. 'Remember, you are now fishermen and not members of the armed forces. Destroy this as soon as you have read and memorised the contents.' He shook hands with both men. The major and sergeant stood up saluted the brigadier and then he strode out of the office, leaving the two men, for the moment, speechless.

Sergeant Symons leaned back to stretch out his arms and almost tipped over the old wicker chair.

Major Bennington disconcertedly fingered the sealed envelope in his hands.

'The top brass must be getting worried, sir.' Symons was disappointed. He was itching to be involved in some real action, but this mission was not what he had been looking for.

'I think you're right Symons. But it also seems that things are not looking too good with the Japs at present. They have both sea and air superiority and are only a jump away from us. I personally find this assignment a little worrying. I hope we will never have to use these caches.'

'It all seems a bit pointless sir; I mean, why can't we go and take a pot shot at the Japs ourselves?' Symons sighed.

The major carefully read through the contents of the envelope.

'I'm sure it won't be too long before you do, but in the meantime we have to complete this mission. Look on the bright side: it's a lovely time of year to be up by the lakes.' He leaned back in his chair, 'Somewhere on the Myall Lakes there is a hidden cave, once used by some escaped convicts. We first have to find this cave and then make it secure with a steel door so that the arms and ammunition are safely hidden from the Japanese invaders.'

'How on earth, sir, can we find this cave in the vast area of these lakes? It could take us months to find it.'

'They have given us part of a very old map which covers one section of the lake-side; this should help us to some extent.' The major smiled; he opened a drawer of his desk and pulled out some blank sheets of paper.

'We will I am sure find this cave, so I will start to prepare a list of what we will need to complete this exercise,' he said, 'but first we must find a good-sized shallow draught fishing boat. It must have a large hold for all the gear we'll be taking with us.'

'I think we can find one if we go down to Ulladulla, sir. I have an uncle who owns just the type of boat we need. He used to be a fisherman, but he's injured his back and can't take the boat out any more.'

Symons continued thoughtfully: 'I know at the beginning of the war he put a powerful new diesel engine in the trawler. And we certainly won't need all his fishing gear, so that will give us plenty of storage space in the boat's hold.'

'That sounds like one problem solved, Symons.'

'I gather money is not too much of a problem, sir. It's a fine boat but he will want a good price for it. I suppose paying cash for this boat is part of the cover up of this operation. No paperwork!' He grinned.

'Apparently we have an open purse sergeant, within reason of course. The navy will be taking the boat over when we have finished with it. They must be short of small patrol boats at present. We had better get down there this afternoon, and if we can do a deal, we might be able to bring the trawler up to Sydney tomorrow.'

The major stood up and Symons mirrored him.

'Slip over to the transport section and organise a car for us,' Bennington ordered. 'Someone will have to collect it from Ulladulla later. I hope we will be able to return to Sydney with the boat.'

'What time do we need the car for, sir?'

'Give me two hours to finish my lists. Sergeant, this really is top-secret. I will have to destroy all this paperwork when we are ready to go.'

'Don't we have to account for any of our expenses, sir?'

'This is so secret that I was given a lump sum of money and told to cover all our tracks as we progress. They must trust me! I suppose we were picked because I have had some building experience that might come in handy for constructing doors around this cave, and you have a good knowledge of the lakes and handling boats.'

'Good God, sir; they must be pretty desperate to part with all that money!' Symonds stared down at the large pile of notes on the table.

The major nodded. 'Indeed. And all this money just to find a cave.'

'How do we even know it exists?' asked Symons.

'Someone in the war office found out about it amongst some very old records. They believe the cave was originally dug out by a group of escaped convicts round about 1840, just a short time after the massacre of nearly all the Aboriginal people in the area. They think it's on the side of a hill, overlooking the Bombah Broadwater. So far, no one has ever found it. It's probably totally concealed by undergrowth.'

The major leaned back in his chair smiling and slowly shaking his head.

'It all sounds a bit far-fetched if you don't mind, sir.' Symons chuckled.

'Let's hope there are not too many hills on that side of the lake, Sergeant. When we find it we have been ordered to clean it out, build a secure entrance using the steel doors supplied to us and make absolutely sure it is completely concealed from view.'

'If we do a good enough job, even our own guys won't be able to find it. Surely, this is something for the Sappers; these guys are trained for this sort of work. We should be out in the field fighting the enemy.' Symons was feeling increasingly irritated at the prospect of this seemingly pointless exercise.

'You've missed the point, Sergeant. The reason for this secrecy is that this could be one of Australia's last lines of defence. If the Japanese Army overruns us, which seems quite possible at present, then the only thing left for us to do is to form a guerrilla army. We'll have to place small pockets of resistance in isolated spots around the country which will wear down the Japs and hopefully make it easier for an Allied invasion.' He grunted.

'Yes sir, I see that now. Perhaps you and I could collect a few stragglers and form our own private army. I'd like that.' He beamed.

'And that's more than possible the way the war is going, Sergeant.'

'Well we better get going, sir. It seems we have no time to waste.

The major gave a quick call to the brigadier to inform him of their intended purchase of a fishing boat at Ulladulla and then followed the sergeant down to the car pound.

George Symons, once a big man with the power of an ox, now walked with a stick, his clothes hanging loosely form his shrunken body. He shook hands vigorously with the major and gave his nephew, Anthony Symons, a powerful bear hug. Ever since the drowning of his brother, George had treated Tony as his son and a strong bond had developed between them.

Tony and his father had been out trawling on his father's fishing boat, which often happened during school holidays. There has been a strong wind earlier that day and the sea was still quite choppy. Tony was steering the boat and his father was standing in the stern-end getting ready to winch in the trawl net.

At that very moment the trawl became caught-up in a large submerged object, the forward movement achieved by the trawler's powerful engine pulled down the stern of the trawler; at the same time the trawler was hit by an extra-large freak wave. Tony cut the engine but it was too late, the trawler was swamped as the water poured in over the stern, resulting in the rapid sinking of the trawler.

Tony found himself swimming surrounded by bit of debris which had floated up from the sunken trawler – but there was no sign of his father. Tony as usual, had just been wearing shorts and tea shirt, but his father had been dressed in oil-skins and long heavy rubber boots.

Fortunately another trawler had been within sight of the now sunken trawler and the skipper had headed to where he could see the floating debris. On the way he pulled in his trawl and was soon able to pick up Tony, who luckily was a strong swimmer.

After several hours searching the area, the trawler returned to Ulladulla where George was waiting to console his nephew. From that time onwards, Tony was adopted by his uncle and the strong bond established between them.

'So you want me to sell my fishing boat, Tony. You have been able to skipper it a few times, under my supervision of course and you know, had you wanted to take up fishing, the boat would have been yours. However, if it is going to be used to help the war effort, it will be taking my place in serving Australia. Maybe it will help bring an end to this bloody war.' He paused and grinned. 'And you are going to pay me for it?'

'Look George, it's just perfect for us. I will organise the payment. You might even get lucky and be able to buy it back cheaply from the Government after the war. Do you fancy coming up to Sydney with us, just to show us the ropes?' The major turned to his sergeant, 'Your uncle can check you out and maybe you can buy the boat from him after the war.'

George's face lit up. 'That really would be great, Major. I can show you a few tricks on the way; she really is a great sea boat, but like a good woman needs a firm hand at times.'

'Good. I will organise someone to bring you back home once we're finished in Sydney.' He paused for a moment. 'George, you wouldn't have any old fishing clothes about the place would you? We need to get out of these uniforms.'

'No problem, mate. There is a whole drawer full of old clothes below that I am sure will fit both of you. The lads left them when they went off to join the navy. So what are you boys up to? Are you going to spy on the Japs?'

The major just smiled, held his finger to his nose and winked.

He walked over to the harbour office, where two Australian Navy officers controlled the movements of the locally stationed patrol boats and the few remaining fishing boats. An elderly sea captain greeted him.

'Welcome Major Bennington, we've been expecting you. We received notification from the War Office; all we need from you is the registration number of your boat. Apparently, there is to be no paperwork involved. This must be something rather special.'

'You're right there, Captain. The registration number painted on the trawler is A-UDOPM. If we are challenged, do we use this number?'

'Yes. Sydney Harbour and the coastal defence outposts between Ulladulla and Sydney have been notified of the trawler's route. You'll be met and escorted into Sydney Harbour.'

★

Dressed in the clothes George had given them, the two soldiers looked more like a couple of down and outs than fishermen when they set off from Ulladulla just before four o'clock the next morning. It turned out to be a bumpy trip, but with the powerful motor and George's good advice, the boat ploughed its way through the heavy seas.

They were met by a launch a mile outside the Heads, the entrance to Sydney Harbour; they followed the escort launch through the anti-submarine nets and tied up at a vacant pontoon in Manly Harbour at eight-thirty that evening. After a hot meal and a few pints of beer, they settled down for the night in the spacious main cabin that boasted two bunks each side and a large table with forms, all attached to the deck in the centre of the cabin.

A ladder led up to the enclosed bridge, the galley was on one side of the ladder and on the other side the toilet and a washbasin. Behind the ladder, a door with a flight of steps led down to the engine room.

The trawler had a large after-deck, with a powerful winch for hauling in the trawl nets and a large hold for storage. Behind the bridge was a small but sturdy-looking lifeboat, complete with a derrick for launching the lifeboat. Ahead of the bridge on the foredeck, was a square hatch giving access to another fair-sized hold, used mainly for fish and fishing tackle storage.

The next morning, the major was able to organise a lift to take George back to Ulladulla. It was an emotional parting for George, as he did not expect to see his boat or his nephew again. As soon as he had gone, the major went into Manly to order all the building materials that they would need for the construction work.

Shortly after, a truck arrived with a load of sand and

gravel, which they laboriously transferred to the boat's hold. Another truck with cement, a cement mixer, wheelbarrows, spades and shovels and some wide planks of timber followed it.

Sergeant Symons realised that there was a possible danger that the sand and gravel might shift in a rough sea and so upset the balance of the trawler. He placed the bags of cement on top of all the sand and gravel then spread and tied down a tarpaulin sheet.

'Looks like you and I have some hard slog ahead of us, Sergeant. I think it is time for a few pints; we'll be making an early start in the morning. Since we're out of uniform, we can forget rank for tonight.'

It was just before dawn when an army truck arrived with two heavy steel doors and a cast iron doorframe. It took all the strength of the four soldiers and their sergeant to lift the doors and frame, and then lower them carefully on to the deck of the trawler.

'These are your building instructions, sir.' The sergeant handed the major a leather briefcase. Before the soldiers climbed back on to the truck, they passed down six pipe rollers and a heavy block and tackle, for moving the doors and frame, also five cases of army food supplies.

The sergeant climbed into the cab. 'We can't stop sir; we are off to Brisbane, and we should be there by tomorrow night.' He smiled as they moved off. 'All go, sir!' he shouted.

The two men then carefully stowed away all the supplies in the after hold of the trawler.

'Well, that's it, Sergeant. Why don't we go to the shops and get some decent supplies? We don't have to just live on what the army gives us.'

'How about the arms and ammunition sir?'

'At midnight we will be escorted to a jetty at the submarine base on the north side of the harbour. We will move over to the fuel pontoon and top up the fuel tank. If we take on a dozen jerry cans of fuel and a supply of petrol for the mixer, we should have enough fuel on board to last for the whole exercise.'

'We can store all the arms in the small hold on the after deck, with the other supplies. We'll then be escorted through the minefields and anti-submarine nets until we are well clear of the Sydney Harbour entrance.'

★

At three am, with a light onshore breeze, they ploughed their way through rough seas, passing out through the Sydney Harbour heads.

Both men were experienced in handling small boats, the major on his father's yacht during the school holidays and Sergeant Symons on his uncle's trawler in Ulladulla.

'Looks like a bit of a slop out there, sir.' The two men could see the occasional wave breaking farther out to sea. Once they were out beyond the heads, the escort vessel turned and headed back to the harbour entrance. The combination of an on-shore wind and ebb tide created a rough sea with an occasionally extra-large wave soaking the deck with spray.

They were both standing in the well-sheltered and spacious wheelhouse. Symonds swung the bow of the trawler into the oncoming waves. The deck was now covered in spray each time a large wave hit the bow of the trawler.

'Look, Sergeant,' began Major Bennington. 'Since we are going to spend a lot of time together, possibly months, and we seem to get on well, let's drop rank formalities for the remainder of this exercise. Besides, it'll help us conceal our identity if we are ever in the company of civilians.'

'As you wish, sir. Whilst we are out of uniform I presume, sir?'

'So long as you remember I give the orders.' Bennington smiled.

'Right. So until we have finished this job, it's Jim and Tony.' Jim leaned across the steering wheel and gave Tony's hand a quick shake. 'Good-day, Tony old boy!'

'And good morning to you Jim – sir … old boy!' Tony laughed.

'There's quite a difference in the way she's meeting the waves, sir – I mean, Jim. I think maybe she is just a little overloaded. She is certainly much lower in the water this time.'

'Not really surprising. Allowing for the tides, we should make an average speed of seven knots. It would take us about fourteen hours to get to Port Stephens, but I don't think it's a good idea for us to travel by night, so let's go into Broken Bay. That's about four hours from here. We can shelter for the night at Pittwater and make an early start in the morning.'

'That sounds good to me, Jim. We'll be turning north soon and the seas will be on our starboard beam. That means we will be rolling a lot, and I'm a bit worried about the sand and gravel shifting in the hold.'

'I think you are right, Tony. That's another good reason for going into Broken Bay. Try easing her around to the north a little; now that we are farther out to sea the waves might be more in our favour.'

For the next three hours, the trawler ploughed its way up north without any great problem. However, when they turned to head in to Broken Bay, the mouth of the Hawkesbury River, they soon found that they were in very rough and broken seas. One minute they were almost surfing the crest of large waves with the bow sometimes disappearing in clouds of spray and then they were battered by large cross-waves which rolled the trawler from one side to the other. Jim wedged himself in one corner of the wheelhouse whilst Tony clutched the wheel, using all his strength to keep the trawler on course.

'We're listing to port, Jim. The cargo has shifted. I think we are in deep shit.' Tony yelled whilst straining to keep the trawler on course. His arms were aching with constant turning of the wheel.

Jim moved over and grabbed the wheel. 'Take a break and look ahead. I think we are almost through this sea.'

Sure enough, minutes later and listing badly, they found themselves in much calmer water and headed into the quiet waters of Pittwater behind Palm Beach. After dropping the anchor a hundred yards out from the jetty, Jim went below and returned a few minutes later with a loaf of bread, a hunk of cheese and two bottles of beer.

The men later found that water had seeped into the hold, making it much harder to shovel the gravel. It was almost dark when they finished levelling the sand and gravel. They replaced the cement bags, and checked the lashing on the steel door and frame, on the deck.

Too tired to cook a meal, they opened a tin of bully beef and finished the loaf of bread, washing it down with a couple of bottles of beer and then turned in for a few hours' sleep.

At five o'clock the next morning, Tony and Jim set off for Port Stephens. It was a bright cloudless day and the seas had died down, making it an easy run up the coast.

Some hours later, they entered the Port Stephens' waterway passing the prominent Yacaaba Head hill on their right.

'It looks like an American ship anchored over the other side of the harbour at Nelson Point,' said Tony.

'I'm sure it will be the first of many. This harbour will make an ideal base for the American Navy; let's hope they get here before the Japs.'

After a short run to the mouth of the Myall River, they followed the markers up to Tea Gardens, the small village a short way up the river on the left side, passing a busy saw mill on the right-hand side of the river. At four thirty, they tied up at the wharf opposite the local pub at Tea Gardens and after a brief rest, Jim went looking for a shop where he was able to stock up with fresh bread and milk, which would last them a few days once they reached the lakes. He also found a detailed tourist map of the river and lakes, which he quickly slipped into his pocket.

Stretched out on the forward deck in threadbare shorts, Tony was enjoying the afternoon sun. The lack of sleep was catching up with them both.

'I'm worried about arousing the curiosity of the locals, especially the fishermen,' said Jim. 'They most likely think we intend to move in on their territory. Let's go up the river until we are well past the village, find a quiet spot and anchor for the night.'

Tony stood up and leisurely stretched himself. 'You don't think we can make the lake before dark?'

'It is at least four hours' motoring, that is providing we don't run aground too often; I have been told that it's not an easy river to navigate as there are shallow areas, and the river twists and turns all the way up to the lake.'

Jim rolled himself a cigarette as he watched three pelicans swim majestically past the boat. Tony passed him his lighter.

'We also need to go up on the flood tide, just in case we run aground,' said Jim after some thought. 'We want as few

15

people as possible to notice us. Most of the fishermen who lived along the riverbanks have gone; the young ones have joined up and the older ones are now mostly involved in the local defence force. I checked up on the local tide times and our best time to start is just before dawn; we should get to the lake between seven and eight in the morning.'

Forty minutes later, they dropped anchor in a quiet creek off the river, five miles north of Tea Gardens. Tony found one of his uncle's fishing rods in the wheelhouse and with a small piece of meat from their supplies started to fish off the side of the boat. It was a beautiful quiet evening, except for bird cries and the occasional plop, as a fish jumped out of the water.

Tony was beginning to lose interest when suddenly his line went taut. 'I've got one!' he yelled and quickly landed a good-sized black bream, followed by two more. 'That's our supper, Jim; better get the spuds on. I'm starving.'

At dawn the next morning they hauled the anchor up and headed up the river. The sky was overcast; a light rain started, which became heavy for the rest of their journey.

'This is really good,' remarked Jim. 'It will keep the inquisitive people indoors for a while.'

Jim managed to keep the boat in deep water all the way up the beautiful winding river, occasionally passing green paddocks, but mostly trees with their leafy branches reaching right down to the water. At one point near the top end of the river they passed a number of apparently deserted old fisherman's cottages partly hidden by the trees.

They arrived at the lake just after seven; the water stretched out in front of them a glassy surface as far as they could see. They passed a line of trees and some tall reeds that appeared to be growing out of the water; it was in fact a tiny island about three hundred yards from the entrance to the river.

The rain had stopped and there were now large patches of blue sky. There was not the slightest ripple on the surface of the lake. Tony gave the engine full throttle and the trawler's bow wave cut through the surface of the water leaving a large area of disturbed water astern.

'Do you know that the total area of all these connecting lakes covers almost twenty-five thousand acres and is surrounded by almost the same acreage of forest? That was, I noticed, mentioned in tourist map.'

'It all seems so unreal here,' replied Tony. 'It gives me a strange feeling, as if I'm in some sort of mysterious land on another planet. It's so quiet. You wonder if there's any life in these surrounding forests.'

'I agree. There's not a single boat or human being in sight. It feels as if time has stopped.' Jim looked down at his watch, just to check that it hadn't.

'I think we'll head south west, Tony. This hidden cave is somewhere on the south side of this lake; but first we need to find a place where we can keep the trawler and ourselves out of sight from passing fishing boats and any of the other vessels that might be going to and from the old sawmills. I believe there is a place called Dirty Water Cove which used to have a sawmill close-by.'

'Taken from your map as well, Jim? It doesn't sound a very nice sort of place.'

They motored all the way along the south side of the lake, unable to get close to the lakeside, the water being far too shallow. On reaching the point where the lake narrowed and which would take them on to Dirty Water, they turned and started to head back towards the river entrance.

'Maybe we should be looking for a hillside with a stream running down its side,' Tony suggested. 'A stream like that would carry a lot of water and would flow down into the lake, and, over a long period of time, create a channel of deeper water.'

'That's brilliant, Tony! Go get me the binoculars.' Jim slowed the engine so that the boat just drifted slowly along. They both scoured the small passing hillsides, looking for a mountain stream.

They were almost halfway back to the river, when they both noticed some moving specks of white. It was a stream of water running down from an especially tall hill. Jim stopped the engine and scanned the hillside with his binoculars.

'It certainly looks like a fast running stream, Jim.'

'It's a stream all right but it disappears before reaching the tree tops; there must be another small hill, in front of the hill with the stream.'

'Why don't we go in closer?' said Tony. 'We can drop the anchor, then take the lifeboat and explore this place.'

The two men were able go quite a way in towards the lakeside before dropping anchor. They quickly lowered the lifeboat, which immediately started to leak.

'It's been out of the water too long but the wood will soon swell and the leaking will stop. I think we can leave it in the water now.' Jim fixed up a lead line to check the depth of the water, and jumped down into the leaking boat. Tony threw a bucket into the lifeboat and joined Jim.

The bottom of the lake was pure white sand and the water crystal clear, but there were also large areas that contained a mixture of tall grass and seaweed that covered the sand. They soon found a clean underwater area that ran up towards the point where the exit of the stream could be.

'This is the channel,' declared Jim. 'It's much deeper here. Over the years, water from the stream has washed away the sandy bottom.'

They followed this channel right up to the side of the lake and then to their surprise, they discovered a narrow entrance with tall reeds on either side, which led into a small but deep lagoon. Just inside this lagoon, almost hidden by the overhanging branches of the paperbark and swamp oak trees, water from the previous night's rain was flooding in.

'This is perfect,' said Jim. 'The channel is deep enough to bring the trawler right into this lagoon so now we will be hidden from the prying eyes of passing fishermen.'

They returned to the trawler and slowly edged it up through the narrow channel until they were able to drop the anchor in the middle of the hidden lagoon.

Standing on the deck they silently admired the pristine landscape. A dense forest covered the hills surrounding them, with a mixture of paperbarks and swamp mahogany, sweet scented wattle and banksia; starting from the top of the brush-covered hills and running right down the side of the hills to the water's edge.

'What a perfect spot,' Jim sighed.

'Yes, but it's a bit noisy; all those birds, ducks and fish plopping in and out of the water.' Tony laughed.

'It's a bird watcher's paradise, Tony. Just on the water, I can see crested grebe ducks, purple swamphens, pelicans, a white egret, little black cormorants and just coming into the lagoon, look, a majestic pair of black swans!'

'Okay Jim, spare me the ornithology for now; but you are right. This is a rather special place.' He stared up at the surrounding hillsides. 'I wonder how close we are to that cave.'

'I would say pretty close,' Jim replied. 'We're about halfway down this side of the lake; this is a well-hidden spot, so I wouldn't be surprised if the cave was somewhere in these hills and close to this lagoon.'

'If we find it that easily,' Tony laughed. 'We will have been very lucky. So how about a couple of beers, a good cooked meal and an early start in the morning.'

'Sounds good. You're the cook, Tony. 'I'm going to bail out the lifeboat; it should have stopped leaking by the morning. We'll row all along the edge of the lake to see if we can see some traces of an old track running down to the water's edge.'

'If not, we will have to put on our heavy boots, thorn-proof clothes and just work our way backwards and forwards across the side of the lake until we reach the top.' Tony groaned. 'That could take weeks.'

They set off early the next morning. The wooden boards of the lifeboat had swelled overnight so there was no need to bail it out. They slowly rowed around the edge of the lagoon and then out along the bank of the lake, all the way back until they were almost at the river entrance. It was dark by the time they got back to the trawler.

'Well, that was a nice easy day,' Jim remarked as they sat drinking a well-earned beer on the deck of the trawler. 'A perfect day. Tomorrow onwards will be hard work as we will have to cut our way through some parts of the bush, if we want to do a thorough job.'

'We can't possibly cover the whole side of the lake, Jim.'

'I feel this is a likely place close to this lagoon. So we will work across an area one mile either side of the lagoon.' Jim stood up, stretched and headed for the galley. 'I'll do the cooking tonight.'

For the next few days, they covered the area to the left of the stream, travelling one mile backwards and then forwards at ten-yard intervals, leaving fallen twigs as markers to cover the parts they searched. At times, they had to cut their way through thick bushes, always on the lookout for poisonous snakes, which were quite numerous in that part of the world. On their return, with the aid of a pair of tweezers they had to spend time removing the ticks from their legs.

It was a fruitless and tiring search; they decided to take a day's rest before searching to the right of the stream. That evening, standing on the deck enjoying a beer, they suddenly heard a long mournful howl coming from the hillside.

'That's a dingo calling his mate, and not too far away.' Tony stared up at the hillside but the animal was well hidden in the thick undergrowth.

'We will have to be a bit careful. The males can be quite aggressive especially if the female is close by with her pups.'

The next day they set off to search the area to the right of the stream. This proved even more difficult as the semi-swampland was a mixture of tall reeds, swamp mahoganies, paperbarks and cabbage tree palms that stretched a fair way inland, to the closed canopy of tea trees, swamp oaks and gum trees.

Four days later, they were only halfway up the hillside, with still no sign of any track that might lead them to the cave.

'If I wanted a safe hiding place, I would want a hideout close to a stream and high enough up the hillside to give me a good vision of the lake,' Jim mused. 'Also the stream would be the footpath leaving no traces of foot prints.'

'You're right; we should have done that in the first place. It's certainly worth a try.'

It was a full moon and the normally quiet night was interrupted, by the cries and howls of several dingoes. At first light, Jim and Tony set off and started their climb up the hillside stream. By midday, they reached the top of the tree level where thick bush covered the rest of the hillside. The stream was now just a small trickle. Tony happened to turn around and look down-stream. A large light-brown dingo was standing in the water, watching them.

'Look, we're being followed.' Tony laughed.

'He's a big fellow, isn't he? Maybe we're approaching his lair. He could get quite aggressive. I'm glad we have our sticks with us. See if he follows us.'

As they continued up the stream, the dingo maintained a steady distance behind them. They finally arrived at a point where a large bush covered the side of the stream. They heard a yelp and turned to see the dingo racing towards them. As it reached them, it leaped in the air aiming for Tony's throat. Tony stepped aside – the dingo turned and grabbed Jim's lower leg – Tony brought his stick down hard on the dingo's back – it swung around to attack Tony; now both men were lashing out at the frenzied animal.

After several blows from Tony and Jim, the dingo finally turned away and slowly limped a few yards upstream.

'You okay, Jim? Lucky we both had sticks with us.'

'My trousers suffered, but I think my leg is only bruised. His family must be living inside that bush. Let's take a look, but you watch out for him. He might come back for a second round.'

Jim crossed over to the tangle of banksia and bottlebrush and pulled back some of the thick foliage. 'It's here!' he yelled. 'We've found it. The cave is right here!' A loud growling noise came out of the narrow cave entrance where the female dingo was protecting her young.

At the same time, the male dingo started to come back towards them ready to continue the fight to save his family. The dingo yelped as Tony struck him on his neck. 'Look behind you, Jim,' he yelled.

Jim turned to see the mother and two pups. They had quietly come out from the cave and were creeping through the bushes.

The dingo bitch stood there staring at Jim and then she slowly walked up to the stream followed by her two young pups; she turned and for a brief moment stared sadly at Jim. She would now have to find another home far from these strange cruel people.

The male dingo gave several high-pitched yelps, and then followed his family upstream until they disappeared into the bush.

'Well, thanks to the dingo, we have found the cave. But I do feel sorry for his family.' Jim sighed.

'No need to worry about them, Jim. They'll soon find another lair. They should be happy they were able to serve their country in such a noble way.' Tony grinned and pulled back a leafy branch of the overhanging bush.

'Well, let's see what we have here. It's a pretty narrow entrance.'

The cave entrance was situated beneath a several yard long strip of rock. A thick layer of dirt covered the overhanging rock, enabling the bushes to grow right over and completely cover the entrance to the cave. Over the years, dirt and fallen leaves had built up in front of the cave, leaving only the small entrance, enabling the dingoes to enter and establish their lair.

Jim squeezed in as far as he could and peered into the dark cave. 'It looks pretty big inside. Hard to see much in the dark.'

'We better go and fetch picks and shovels, and a gun in case the dingo's decided to come back.'

'You won't see dingoes once we have dug out the entrance, Tony.

'It's not worth coming back today but we must make an early start in the morning.'

★

There was no sign of the dingoes in the morning and the two men started to clear away the large mound of dirt that had built up in front of the cave.

The next day, they uncovered a heap of stones, the remains of a wall, which the old convicts must have built to protect themselves from the many wild creatures that inhabited the forest in those days.

They would have to move the stones to one side in order to bring in the iron door and frame.

As soon as they were able, they climbed over the stones and explored the inside of the cave. It was ten yards deep and five wide. It had an uneven rock ceiling, which varied between seven and nine feet high. The sides and back of the cave were a mixture of solid rock and shale; the convicts had obviously extended it. The only sign of habitation was blackened stones, where they had made their fire. The floor was surprisingly dry and covered with a layer of white sand, which the convicts must have brought into the cave.

It took the two men several days of hard digging to clear enough space to bring in and fit the doorframe and then it rained for several more days, making it impossible to drag the doors up the stream.

They spent the wet days preparing the block and tackle, ready to haul the heavy door and frame up through the stream.

'We can use some of the timber to make a carriage to hold the door and frame upright,' said Jim. 'That way, it will be able to slide over the rollers.'

'Good idea, Jim; that will leave us both free to heave on the block and tackle. But it means we will have to keep stopping every few yards to move the rollers forward.'

They decided use the trawler's derrick to lift the frame from the deck of the trawler and lower it down on to the lifeboat. This proved to be a delicate operation as the frame overhung both sides of the lifeboat and threatened to capsize it.

It took a whole day to get the doorframe, the door and the carriage onto the bank alongside the stream. After a while, having completed all the work on the trawler, tempers started to fray, so the men decided to take the lifeboat out on to the lake and do some fishing.

They stayed close to the shore, in case any other boats came by and they had to take cover under the overhanging branches that were growing along the edge of the lake. This proved very successful; Tony was in his element and he soon had a good catch of flatheads and black bream.

When at last the sun came out, they started to haul the doorframe up the stream. They manhandled the carriage on to the rollers, which rested on the stony bottom of the stream, drove a heavy stake higher up the stream, attached the block and tackle to the stake and were able to both pull the skid to the end of the rollers. They then moved the rollers up in front of the skid and gradually pulled the doorframe up the stream without it falling over.

This operation took three days as on several occasions when they encountered a slight bend in the stream, the frame fell over and it took a painstaking amount of time to get it upright again.

They repeated the operation with the metal door. This was much easier as it lay flat on the carriage. It only took two days to haul it to the cave. Having fixed the doorframe in position, they then hauled up bags of cement and gravel in a wooden box, which they fitted to the carriage.

With the doorframe in place they worked together building up a solid wall that closed in the front of the cave and were at last able to fit the iron door in place. The next job was to replace all the dirt and stones to conceal the wall they had built, with just a narrow passage leading to the door of the cave.

Their last job was to carry all the arms and ammunition up to the cave and carefully store them on the dry sand at the back of the cave.

'Some of these cases feel too heavy to be ammunition cases,' remarked Tony. 'I wonder if there is something else in them. They also have metal bands around them; that's a bit unusual, isn't it?'

'That's not our concern. We just do our job and that's the end of it. If there is something different in some of these cases then they have made sure we don't open them. So just forget it, Tony.'

Jim had his own ideas about the cases, but was not going to mention this to Tony. Their job was now over and that was all that mattered.

Finally, Jim ceremonially closed the door and slid the three bolts across.

'Unfortunately we cannot padlock this door because if any resistance people come here, they certainly won't have a key to open it. Padlocks would not be a problem to any unauthorised person, so we just have to rely on our ability to cover-up any traces of this cave.'

'So how the hell will they know where the arms are stored, Jim?'

'I suppose you and I will have to draw up some maps which they'll issue to the resistance leaders if and when the time comes.' Jim sighed. 'That's not our worry, anyway. At least you and I will be able to find the cave, if we are still around.'

Both satisfied and relieved at a job well done, they stood to attention and saluted the bolted door.

'Good luck to this bunker and all who fight from it.' Tony laughed.

'And let us hope it will never be needed,' Jim added.

That night, Major James Bennington and Sergeant Anthony Symons got very drunk celebrating a completed mission, both blissfully unaware of the events that were to follow.

'We need to spend all day tomorrow tidying up in front of the bunker and then we can work all the way down the stream and along the edge of the lake. We must cover all our foot marks and also try to repair the damage to the foliage and flattened reeds.' Jim stood up, yawned and slowly headed for his bunk.

'If we set off for Sydney shortly after midnight tomorrow, we should arrive at the entrance to Sydney Harbour by early evening the next day. Actually, I am a bit worried about that. We could run into problems identifying ourselves and we don't want to be fired at by our own people.'

Mindful of the importance of covering all traces of their mission, Tony and Jim had always been extremely careful not to leave too many footprints. Every few days they carefully scraped and levelled the soil leaving little to do at the end of their mission.

So on the last day, starting from the bunker, now well concealed by the overhanging bushes, they slowly worked their way down the stream until they got to the water's edge, wiping out all traces of their presence as they went.

It was late afternoon when they finally rowed out to the trawler, satisfied that no inquisitive local fishermen could possibly see any trace of their presence there.

'There is only a little scattered cloud and also it's a full moon, so we will set off well after dark,' Jim said. 'The locals living on the side of the river will all be sleeping and there should be sufficient light for us to navigate down the river and out to the ocean well before dawn.' He smiled. 'So let's use up lots of our food supplies and have a really good last meal tonight.'

'Great idea, Jim. I'll let you cook it.' Tony laughed. 'So I suppose we'll be in Sydney by this time tomorrow catching up on all the war news.'

'On reflection,' said Jim thoughtfully, 'I think we had better give Sydney a miss and go straight down to Ulladulla.'

Tony looked disappointed. 'Why is that? I was hoping for a night out when we get back to Sydney.'

'We have no means of communicating with Sydney and we might run into trouble if we try to enter the harbour. It's possible that all the anti-submarine nets are now in place. Anyway, it will attract less attention as we will be just another trawler returning to Ulladulla from a fishing trip.'

At one o'clock, they had lifted the anchor and were crossing the lake to the head of the river. With just enough light and the engine ticking over, they drifted downstream. By five o'clock they slowly passed Tea Gardens and half an hour later had arrived at the Port Stephens' waterway.

Tony, having studied the charts of Port Stephens, kept the trawler close to the north side, risking the shallow water rather than the chance of being spotted by the three American ships now anchored at Nelson Bay on the south side of the Port Stephens' waterway.

At six o'clock, following three other fishing boats, they passed between Yacaaba Head and Tomaree Head and then out into the ocean. The other three fishing boats turned to the north whilst they continued east for the next hour, before heading south for Ulladulla.

The trawler was just over ten miles from the now distant Australian coast. It was a fine clear morning with an almost calm sea. The engine was running smoothly with the bow of the trawler cutting through the water, giving them a steady eight knots.

'This is a perfect end to a very successful operation, sir. It's strange, when you think about it: we are the only people that know where the arms are hidden.'

'Thanks to both our efforts, we have been able to complete our mission successfully and in good time. But yes, you are quite right Sergeant, because we are not allowed any radio contact, no one knows where we are and until we meet up with the brigadier, the hidden arms remain our secret. Interesting.'

The major continued. 'It is a puzzling situation, I don't think you and I have seen the last of that bunker. I have a feeling you and I will either be returning one day with other resistance people to make use of those arms, or hopefully will return to remove the arms from the bunker when the danger from Japan is over.'

The major was silent for a moment.

'Look Tony, I'm afraid we have to return to our respective ranks again. It's really good that we have got on so well together. If we don't meet up at the bunker again, I just hope we will meet up when the war is over.'

'I would like that very much, sir; I hope we will be able to go fishing again when all this is over.'

'Look sir; we have company.' A shoal of dolphins were running on both sides of the trawler, as if to give them a safe escort down the coast.

'Yes, Sergeant. And we have more company coming up behind us on our Port side,' the major calmly murmured. 'I just hope it's one of ours.'

The periscope soon turned into a large wave as the submarine broke surface; the Japanese flag was flying from behind the periscope. Several of the crew scrambled out on to the deck of the submarine and manned the gun on the after deck.

'Oh my God!' Tony exclaimed. 'And we are completely unarmed. Shall I turn in towards the shore, sir?'

Those were his last words as the first shell struck the trawler, followed by two more direct hits on the vessel's bridge that killed both men.

Several minutes later, the trawler slowly disappeared under the water leaving a patch of oil, a few odd bits of timber and two dead bodies.

The submarine, with just its periscope showing, headed farther out to sea. Very soon after, the sharks moved in, until nothing remained of the two brave men.

★

The following night, several mini submarines entered Sydney Harbour, causing considerable damage and loss of life. Among those killed in Sydney that night were Brigadier Nollybenn and his driver.

The previous day, an aircraft had spotted floating oil,

life jackets, several pieces of timber and debris while out on routine patrol near the Newcastle area. Since no fishing boats had been reported missing, this information had been passed on to Brigadier Nollybenn, who, it was known, had been waiting to hear if there was any news of his special secret mission.

The brigadier and his driver had driven up to Sydney to find out if there was any further information regarding Major Bennington and his sergeant. Unfortunately for them, they arrived at the naval dockyard just at the moment when the Japanese submarines started making their attack on Sydney Harbour.

They were driving along a wharf when a shell exploded close by. The driver was hit by a piece of flying shrapnel and the car ran out of control, driving straight over the end of the wharf and disappeared into the deep water with the two men trapped inside.

With the deaths of Brigadier Nollybenn, Major Bennington and Sergeant Symons, the whereabouts of the cave containing the arms, ammunition and gold bullion were not only lost, but because the security established by the brigadier was so efficient, in the hectic months that followed, this hidden cache of arms was completely overlooked and forgotten.

CHAPTER 2

In perfect line ahead, they quietly made their way, passing through the still waters of the harbour entrance, as they slowly glided to the centre of the glassy surface of the small harbour.

As if by order from their leader, they broke away from the line but then spread out, forming a large circle in the centre of the harbour.

The black swans had arrived.

Marçel looked on transfixed as they started to explore the quiet waters, dipping between and ringing around a number of moored yachts which belonged to the inhabitants of the village of Nerong, once called Dirty Water Cove.

With hardly a ripple, they glided on the still and dark water. Every now and then, a head would disappear under the surface and re-emerge with a morsel of weed in its bill. Over many years, tea-tree oil from the dead leaves falling from the trees into the lake had stained the water a light-brown colour, leaving it murky and opaque.

The reflection of the yachts, houseboats and all the waterfront houses on the mirror-like surface of the water gave the false impression of an extremely crowded harbour and then, with a slight puff of wind to ruffle its surface, the picture quickly changed.

Standing on the stone jetty, Marçel watched as one particularly large black swan headed gracefully in his direction. Unlike white swans that make a loud hissing noise, black swans emit a soft trumpeting sound. Marçel heard the bird call as it drifted towards him.

The swan was quite close to him when it suddenly stopped. Its head and neck disappeared under the dark water, and re-appeared holding something white – a human hand – in its large yellow and red-tipped bill.

The swan then turned and swam back out towards the centre of the harbour, dropping the white hand and letting it sink back down into the muddy depths.

Marçel stepped back, shocked at what he had seen. Had the swan really been holding a human hand in its bill?

He watched as the black swan re-joined its bevy which then glided in unison out of the harbour and out on to the enormous Great Lakes.

Uncertain of what to do, Marçel looked around to see if anyone else had been watching the swan but there was no one in sight. Should he report it to the police or just continue on his way?

Marçel had been driving down from the Gold Coast in Queensland and was on his way to the Sydney Airport, from where he was due to fly back to London the following morning. The last thing he wanted right now was to get involved with a long police inquiry, as this could mean missing his flight and spending several extra days wading through official bureaucracy.

It had happened so fast; what had appeared to him for a matter of seconds to be a human hand could easily have been a white plastic bag. If the police combed the lakebed and didn't find a body, he would not only feel stupid, he might also be accused of wasting valuable police time.

But he was certain that he had seen a human hand.

Marçel got into his car, drove back up the lane and joined the Pacific Highway. With all the heavy traffic on its way down to Sydney from the north of New South Wales and Queensland, he reckoned it would take him at least three hours to get to the airport hotel.

He had planned a good meal and a bottle of wine that evening, followed by a leisurely check-in for his flight at 10 am the next morning. He was due to report for duty to his new chief, Colonel Geoffrey Manderson, just a few hours after arriving in London.

This was a new posting for Marçel; he was joining a little-known section of the British Intelligence Service called M6/V8, which had a small office close to Scotland Yard. Established back in 1941, the section had originally assisted the several underground resistance movements in Europe during the Second World War, and had acted as a liaison between the army and the Metropolitan Police Force.

Marçel had spent six years in the army; the last two were in Afghanistan and Iraq, where he earned his promotion to Captain. Marçel was tall: just a little less than six feet. He'd often been told that his solid build, steel grey eyes, high cheekbones and dark complexion gave him the authoritative air of a leader. It was a look offset by an irrefutably charming boyish smile that also made him attractive to women.

That innocent smile had fooled many people, especially those who had tried to cross him, including the men that had served under him in Afghanistan. Once roused, Marçel became ruthless, and after feeling the lash of his temper, no one dared to stand in his way again.

Unknown to Marçel, Colonel Manderson first noticed him when visiting the army Officers' Training College at Sandhurst. He saw the extraordinary likeness to a Marçel Beaumont whom he had once met at Marçel's winery in Australia. At the time, the old man had talked about his son, Peter, and told him the tragic story of how both Peter and his mother, Marçel Beaumont's wife, had died in a tragic motor accident.

But Marçel Beaumont never mentioned having a grandson.

Later when Manderson returned to London, he studied the file on old Marçel's remarkable career in the department which he, Manderson, had now inherited.

The colonel decided to satisfy his curiosity and find out if the two Beaumonts were connected. Manderson drove down to Rainbury to make further inquiries. He went straight to the village inn, chatted to some of the older inhabitants and learned young Beaumont's history prior to joining the army.

He discovered that the young Captain Marçel Beaumont was born in the small village of Rainbury in Somerset out of wedlock to Minnie Coldwell, an orphan girl who lived and worked on a farm several miles from there.

Peter Beaumont, son of the elderly Marçel Beaumont, stayed at the farm for several nights while on a walking holiday on the moors. Peter was immediately enraptured by the lovely young Minnie, who in her rural innocence was so different from the brash sophisticated girls that he had been grown used to, living in London.

By the end of his stay at the farm, two weeks longer than

originally planned, the couple had fallen in love with each other and decided to get married. It was agreed that Peter would return to Australia to tell his parents and that they would get married as soon as possible after his return to England.

At the village inn, Manderson was told that when the child was born, Minnie was no longer in contact with her boyfriend, Peter. He had gone off to Australia to tell his parents that Minnie was pregnant, but he never returned.

When young Marçel was only one year old, Minnie became seriously ill with cancer. She died a year later, always thinking that Peter had deserted her.

As Minnie did not have any surviving relatives, Marçel Beaumont was taken into care and later adopted by an elderly couple living in the village. Marçel grew up in a loving home with stepparents that adored him. He excelled at school and at seventeen was accepted into the Army Officers Training College at Sandhurst.

His curiosity satisfied, Manderson returned to London and monitored Marcel's career in the army with particular interest.

When Marçel returned from Afghanistan, Colonel Manderson, realising his potential, requested that Marçel be transferred to his department.

His petition was granted, and after their first meeting the two men quickly realised that they had the same determination towards making a better and safer world through their work in the department. An immediate bond was established.

At their second meeting, the colonel revealed to Marcel that he had known Marcel's father, Peter, and his grandfather Marcel Beaumont. He encouraged Peter to take a trip to Australia before starting work with the section, to go and find out about his father and his grandparents.

'Your grandfather was an exceptional man, Marçel,' the colonel told him, now dispensing with formalities. 'I think you will be impressed by what you discover in Australia.'

'I would certainly like to do that.'

'Good. I expect to see you in six weeks' time. Your family is all dead now, but the son of your grandparents' closest friend, Michael Saunders, is still running their winery in the Hunter Valley in New South Wales. I met him by chance there a few years ago.'

'I shall look forward to meeting him and getting to know all the family history.'

'Your grandfather was a great man; he was also a very wealthy man. So, good luck Marçel.'

★

Two days later, Marçel flew out to Sydney. Upon his arrival at the airport, he immediately hired a car and started to drive north. His first call was the Hunter Valley Winery, to meet a Mick Saunders, the son of Father Mick Saunders, who was one of his grandfather's best friends. In turn, Mick had been very close with Marçel's father.

Mick greeted Marçel with the warmth of an old friend. He led his guest through the house to a large balcony with a panoramic view of the vineyard and the Hunter Valley below. Before sitting down he fetched a bottle of wine and two glasses.

'This is one of the best Chardonnay wines we ever produced, Marçel. Isn't it strange that we should meet like this? Neither you nor I realised that the other even existed. Our grandparents were very good friends, you know; your father and I were then best friends and we grew up together.

I never married. I suppose I'm married to the winery.' He laughed.

'So now let's drink to us and from now on may you and I become the best of friends like our fathers.' He studied Marcel's face. 'My God, you look so much like your grandfather.'

Mick went on to describe how he and Peter had grown up together since early boyhood and had gone on to university at Oxford together. 'After graduation, I had no desire to work in England. I was homesick and really was missing Australia, so I returned to work at this winery. My father and Peter's dad worked so hard to establish this place here in the Hunter Valley.'

Mick refilled the two glasses and continued.

'After several wild years in London, Peter joined the diplomatic service; he was doing extremely well at his job and lived a very wild social life with his friends there. He came out here on holiday and then,' Mick paused before continuing, 'the accident happened.'

'They were on their way back from having seen an opera at the Sydney Opera House. That was a terrible night for all of us. It had been raining heavily all that day; there were landslides all over the place and the roads that night were treacherous. They should never have left Sydney.'

'I suppose that was before the freeway was completed, Mick.'

'That's right. The old roads were pretty dangerous at the best of times.'

There was another silence as the two men contemplated the horrific pictures in their imagination. Mick cut through the uncomfortable silence: 'You see, Marçel, Peter had come out to Australia in 1984 to spend a holiday with his parents.

At the time, I felt sure that Peter had something on his mind but for some reason, he was unable to confide in anyone. I now realise that it was the fact that Peter was shortly to become a father. He was your father, Marcel. The tragedy was that because he died that night, no one ever knew about you.' They were both silent again for a few minutes, thinking how different their lives might have been.

'I was born prematurely in December 1984. My father should have come back after the New Year, but my mother was left alone to give birth to me,' Marçel murmured at last, gently tapping the glass-topped table.

'So now that at last I know what really happened, I can forgive him.' Marcel emptied his glass and sat back in the armchair reflecting on the past. He was finally seeing the back of the ghost that had haunted him since childhood.

'You know Marçel, my parents and your grandparents were lifelong friends. After the accident my parents were never quite the same. They died just a few years later, and I'm sure that the shock of the tragedy had something to do with it.'

'It must have been a terrible blow to you all at the time, Mick. But then what happened to my grandfather?

'He was completely shattered. He was convinced that if he had been with them, the accident would never have happened. He blamed himself for their deaths. Quite ridiculous, but grief works like that.'

'At only fifty-eight, he suddenly became an old man. I can still remember seeing the change in him. One day he told my parents that he was leaving. He said he had too many painful memories at the winery and that he just had to get away. He had decided to retire.'

'He actually handed his house and his half-share of the

winery to me and just drove away. It devastated my parents to lose him too.'

'How very sad. Where did he go?'

'Your grandfather bought a house on the Gold Coast in Queensland. He wrote to us occasionally and told us that he spent a lot of his time sailing his small boat, and that he was involved with teaching martial arts to university students.'

'Then one day in 2005 I got a letter saying that he was going to Portugal to help an old friend who had gotten himself into some sort of trouble. Apparently there had been a kidnapping by some Nazi gangsters. It was only much later that I realised he was actually saying goodbye to me.'

'He must have been pretty old by then, no?'

'Uncle Marçel, as I always called him, was around seventy-five I think, but he always kept himself extremely fit. Anyway, after that, I never heard from him again.'

'So what happened to him?'

'Both my parents had been ill for some time; my mother died a month after I got that last letter from Uncle Marçel and my father, heartbroken at losing my mother, died three months later. I was kept busy running the winery and caring for my sick parents, so I didn't have so much time to think about him.'

'Then after the funeral and the settlement of their affairs, I decided to take a break and go to Portugal to see if I could find out what had really happened to Uncle Marçel.'

'Did you find him?'

'I was able to talk to Nelson Biadassaris, the son of Uncle Marçel's old friend Alfonso.' Mick crossed over to the sideboard and came back with a family picture.

'This is Nelson, his wife and two children. He told me

that Alfonso, his father, had died shortly after Uncle Marçel had helped release his two children from their kidnappers.'

Mick paused for a moment giving Marçel time to absorb this information.

'To achieve this, Uncle Marçel had exploded a bomb that killed the kidnappers but also himself. This also saved the Ponte D Luis Bridge in Porto Portugal from being destroyed. Nelson told me the Government officials wanted the whole episode covered up as it could well lead to much more damaging past events coming to light; this could damage diplomatic relations with Britain. So I never got the full details out of Nelson.'

'That's incredible, Mick. So what did you do?'

'Nelson gave me the name of a top official in Porto and arranged a meeting for me. The next day I met with him, and he persuaded me to assist in the cover up of the whole episode. In return, he would give me a DNA sample of Uncle Marçel to take back to Australia as proof that he had died in Portugal.' Mick paused to re-fill their glasses.

'So the official story is, Marçel Beaumont drowned in the Rio Douro River and his identified decomposed remains were buried at Aveiro, next to his old friend Alfonso Biadassaris. And that's the end of the story.'

They both sat quietly for a moment. Mick left the room and returned with a second bottle of wine.

'Poor old Grandpa; what a courageous old man. He died to save his old friend's grandchildren. And the Ponte D Louis bridge of course.'

'Marçel, I still have the DNA sample. I know Uncle Marçel's affairs are not yet settled. As you are the only surviving next of kin, you must go to his solicitors on the Gold Coast and take the sample; I will give you their address.

You should inherit his house on the Gold Coast and quite a large amount of money.' Mick paused for a moment.

'In fact, Marçel, you would have inherited this house that I live in, if Uncle Marçel had known of your existence. I have all the money I will ever need here, so just go for it, Marçel.'

'Thanks Mick. I wouldn't even dream of taking your lovely home from you. My grandfather gave you this home because I'm sure he loved you as a son. I'll be more than happy to inherit his house on the Gold Coast and I expect there might be a few dollars to go with it.' He laughed.

They spent the next few days sampling the great wines of the Hunter Valley; they flew over the mountains in Mick's Cessna 150. They drove down to Newcastle and Nelson Bay and sailed in the very large Port Stephens Harbour. Their friendship firmly in place, Marçel finally set off for the Gold Coast.

Within several weeks, Marçel owned a house on the Gold Coast, and had inherited a small fortune. His grandfather's affairs were now settled, and although he was delighted with the outcome, he was also saddened by the whole affair and ready to return to England to take up his new appointment.

Marçel's route back to Sydney took him through Coffs Harbour, where he spent the night. The next day he was able to go surfing at the golden beach of Port Macquarie.

Mick had gone down to Melbourne to a wine conference, so instead of going to the Hunter Valley Winery, Marcel kept to the highway. It was on his way down through Bulahdelah to Raymond Terrace and then on to the freeway to Sydney, that, quite by chance, he drove off the highway into Nerong, where he first saw the black swans.

★

By late afternoon, Marçel arrived at the airport hotel. After checking in at reception, he bought himself a newspaper and went up to his room to shower and rest before going down to the restaurant for dinner.

Rejuvenated after his shower, Marçel was sitting quietly reading the evening newspaper, when he came across the story of a missing English woman, Sophie Dunalle and an Aboriginal girl.

The Aboriginal girl had last been seen getting into the English woman's car. The same car was later found slightly damaged and abandoned at a camping site on the edge of Bombah Broadwater, north of Port Stephens.

The police were asking for anyone who might have any knowledge of the two women's whereabouts to come forward.

Marçel looked at a tourist map of the area he had picked up at a garage. The area where the girls had gone missing was the same place where he thought he had seen the hand earlier that day. He got up and helped himself to a miniature bottle of whisky from the mini bar.

He now knew he was obliged to report his sighting of the hand to the police, but he would first call Colonel Manderson, as this would obviously delay his return to the department in London.

He had Geoff's home number and without calculating the time difference, he picked up the phone and dialled the number.

A gravelly voice answered his call with a hint of irritation.

'Hello? Who the hell wants me at 4:30 am?'

'Sorry sir, Captain Marçel Beaumont here. I'm afraid I got my times a little mixed up.'

Marçel told Geoff about his sighting of the hand in the black swan's bill at Nerong.

'There's a small natural harbour there on the edge of Lake Bombah in New South Wales. I was driving down from Queensland to Sydney and decided to stop there for a rest.' Marçel heard a groan from Geoff and realised the colonel must think he was telling him some sort of drunken joke.

He continued: 'When I arrived at the Airport Hotel in Sydney, I happened to see an article in the newspaper reporting two missing women in the same area, an Aboriginal girl and an English woman.' Marçel went back to describing his sighting of the hand. 'The swan came very close to me and I'm certain that what I saw was a human hand.'

'That sounds interesting. Marçel, are you quite sure it was a hand?'

'Pretty sure, Geoff; the swan came quite close to me. I will have to report my sighting to the local police, but unfortunately I will get myself involved and I may not be able to return to London for a few days. Or do you think I should just keep quiet and return on tomorrow's flight?'

The colonel was silent for a moment.

'Marçel, I want you to go back to this place, but first report your findings to the local police and then I want you to quietly make your own inquiries and report back to me. Believe it or not, it seems there are a few severed hands around. We have come across two in the London area and one down in Weymouth.'

Marçel felt an icy chill surge through his body.

'Go back to the lakes; be discreet and be careful. We could be dealing with some sort of trans-continental serial killer, or else this could be the work of an international organisation that we have been watching over here for some time.'

'Can you tell me anything more about this possibility? I would like to know what I am dealing with.' Marçel was interested.

'No, I can't. Except that two suspects in a murder inquiry in London have gone missing overseas and their crooked London lawyer, who we know is involved in this organisation, has gone to Australia. There could be a connection, but it's tenuous. Anyway since you are there it might be worth following it up. Cancel your flight to London and call me when you have some information. And just be extra careful, Marçel.'

Marçel chuckled. 'I will have to be as careful as possible not to upset the local police force.'

'And get your times right next time you call me. Good night!' Geoff growled.

Marçel cancelled his flight that night and called the Newcastle Police Headquarters. The next morning he drove to the airport and returned his hire car. He took a taxi into Sydney where he bought himself a second-hand Jeep.

He then drove up to the Newcastle Police Headquarters, where he was told to contact the police station at Raymond Terrace, from where the investigation of the missing girls was being conducted.

At Raymond Terrace, Marçel was interviewed by a Detective Inspector Morrow who had been assigned to the case. Sam Morrow, now in his early thirties, was of similar build to Marçel; he had served in the Australian Army before joining the police force. He had left behind a trail of very attractive girlfriends, but was still unmarried, having decided because of his work and his love of sport, especially cricket, he would remain single.

Marriage, Sam had decided was not for him; well not yet, anyway.

During the interview, Marçel explained his reason for visiting Australia and his whereabouts since his arrival. Mick and the Gold Coast solicitors later verified this. He then went on to describe his sighting of the hand in the lake.

Then to Marçel's surprise, Detective Morrow told him that they had received instructions from the Federal Police in Canberra to allow him to follow their investigations, but he was in no way to interfere with their inquiries. Geoff had certainly not wasted any time in making contact with the people in Canberra: Marçel realised this must be quite a serious international investigation.

'Right, as we will be working close together on this case, I think it's Sam and Marçel, if that's okay with you? Firstly, I would like you to come to Nerong Harbour with me right away as the Police Rescue Team are ready to look for the hand and whatever else they might find down there.'

Marçel, delighted to be working with someone of his own age and experience shook Sam's hand.

'I think it's going to be a pleasure working with you Sam – so what's keeping us?'

Back at the Nerong Harbour, Marçel was able to direct the diver to the exact spot where he had first seen the black swan dive down for the hand. After several hours combing the lake bed, the hand was recovered, but nothing else was found; there was no trace in the lake of a human body.

'I suppose there's not much else we can do today, Marçel,' said Sam after they returned to Raymond Terrace later than afternoon. 'You should go find somewhere to stay. Have a drive around Tea Gardens and Hawks Nest. It's a nice area with lots of accommodation.'

Looking at his tourist map of the area, Marçel decided to take Sam's advice and drove down to Tea Gardens, a small town on the side of the Myall River. The Myall then flows on past Hawks Nest, which is on the opposite bank, and eventually out into the large Port Stephens' waterway.

★

The riverside road was lined with attractive houses, shops and cottages, all with good river views. It would make an excellent place to live, thought Marçel, especially if one owned a boat.

Marçel decided to take the Jeep and explore Hawks Nest. He crossed over the river on the 'Singing Bridge' which replaced the old ferry that had previously joined the two towns. He saw extensive mangroves running down the other side of the river as far as the bridge, observing that the river then finally flowed into the Port Stephens Harbour and eventually out into the Pacific Ocean. The harbour portal was impressive, with high hills on either side of the narrow entrance: the Yacaaba Headland to the north and Tomaree Point to the south.

From outside his hotel at Tea Gardens, Marçel was still able to get a view of the river. Scanning the thick Mangrove forest that spread all the way up and down on the other side of the river, it became obvious to him that he must get himself a boat and explore the river and all the surrounding lakes; he might be able to pick up some clues as to where, when and how the woman died. He also knew it would be a pleasure for him to explore the Great Lakes.

He went back into the hotel and into the public bar. It was fairly crowded and soon Marçel found himself chatting to a few of the locals. He told them that he was on leave from the army, and so had taken the opportunity to explore the east coast of Australia.

'I would like to be able to hire a boat large enough to live

47

on whilst I explore the river and the lakes,' he said, having to shout over the noise of the loud voices in the bar.

A young bearded man passed him a fresh schooner of beer. 'You here to investigate the missing girls?' he demanded.

Marçel laughed. 'I'm a soldier, not a policeman mate. I'm just looking for a boat to explore the lakes.'

'Look mate, the best place to hire a boat to explore the lakes is up at Bulahdelah. That's about forty kilometres up the highway north of Tea Gardens on the Myall River.'

'Thanks mate. I think I'll go there straight away. Same again?'

Marçel got the boatyard telephone number from the barman who phoned the boat hire office with his mobile. He was told they had a number of boats available and if he came straight away they could fix him up today.

Forty minutes later, Marçel was at the Bulahdelah boatyard. He found it just below the Bulahdelah river bridge where there were several large luxury houseboats and motor cruisers for hire.

After looking at the various available vessels, Marçel decided to hire an eight-metre Rivera luxury cruiser, which, with its two powerful Volvo motors, would give him the speed he needed to explore the lakes and the offshore islands at Hawks Nest.

Whilst he was sorting out the paperwork, the manager was called away for a few minutes to talk to one of his staff. Marçel leaned over the counter and looked at the booking sheet. He quickly scribbled down the names and dates of the last two weeks' bookings. Of the four houseboats marked down, the two most recent had already been returned, one was due back that day and another had the word 'sold' written across its entry. He wondered if the police had already checked this out.

When the manager returned, Marçel had completed the paperwork; he paid cash in advance for one month's hire and shook hands with the manager. 'So it's okay to come back here for fuel and I can call you on my mobile if I have any problems with the boat?'

'Marçel, you can come back here and tie up to the jetty anytime. There will always someone around to fill up your fuel and water tanks. There's also a general food-store still open and a very good hardware shop in the village. Tell them Shaun sent you.'

Marçel drove back to the village shops to get supplies for the next few days and then he called in at the Plough Hotel for a quick beer in the very busy bar. Most of the regulars were there as it was the weekly 'Draw Night' and the punters were waiting for the chance to walk off with trays of fresh meat or bottles of wine. Marçel had another schooner of ale; then he went and stocked up his own 'ship's bar' from the adjacent bottle shop.

CHAPTER 3

It was no coincidence that the three men came together on a luxury houseboat moored off an almost deserted campsite on the vast Bombah Broadwater in New South Wales.

But it had been a coincidence that an Englishman, who had recently slipped away from a police raid of a cult meeting in Dorset in the UK, met up with an American, a former Ku Klux Klan member who had just escaped from arrest which would have led to jail and then 'death row' for the brutal killing of an Afro-American.

The Englishman, Paul Blendham was thirty-eight: tall, thin and with slightly greying fair hair. His face gave the impression of someone in authority, but there was something strange about the look on his face and his expression that frequently repelled people.

In fact, Paul was a 'bad egg' who came from a blue-blooded English family. Expelled from his public school for bullying he was, thanks to family influence, allowed to join the army from which he was discharged within months for bad behaviour towards other officers and the men under his command.

The end finally came when he assaulted a senior officer in his regiment. Paul returned to the family estate, shunned by family and friends. He spent most of his time in London where, through a private members club, he joined The Order of the White Cross, a secret society affiliated with the Ku Klux Klan in the USA.

The society had several female members and aside from its deeply racist core, was also involved in aggressive sexual behaviour.

The police eventually raided the society, after having received a tip-off from a disgruntled member. On storming a meeting at a cottage in Dorset, they discovered the tortured body of a young woman. Six people were arrested and charged; only three men received prison sentences and the others were later released.

The man believed to have killed the girl was a Paul Blendham; he escaped during the raid. It was later revealed by the local police that he was flown across the English Channel in a Cessna 150 in the early hours of the morning.

From the isolated farm in Normandy France, Paul was soon able to steal a car. He then drove all the way down to the Mediterranean, close to the Italian border. He bribed a French fisherman to take him by sea across to Italy, close to Naples, where he was able to take refuge among the city's lowlifes. And it was in one of these disreputable bars of Naples' shady underworld that Paul Blendham happened to first meet Kenny Lambton.

In contrast to Paul's privileged upbringing, Kenny had grown up in a violent family; his father was a truckie, a bully of a man who used his son, Kenny, as a punching bag.

Before he had reached the age of ten, Kenny had received a broken nose and on two occasions, broken ribs. Because of the beatings, he suffered from poor hearing for the rest of his life.

Nevertheless Kenny soon learned to defend himself; at twelve he was the toughest kid on the street: each time his father beat him, he would walk down the street and take out his anger on the first unfortunate kid he found. By seventeen, he had grown bigger and stronger than his father. The day came when, after a particularly drunken strike, Kenny hit back at his father and beat the pulp out of him. That day he left home and moved over to New Orleans where he got a job in a bakery. The bakery manager was a longstanding member of the local arm of the Ku Klux Klan and, sensing Kenny's pent-up outrage, invited his employee to attend a couple of meetings with him. Within weeks Kenny was a staunch member, and soon became one of the group's most brutal activists.

One night during a vicious attack at an isolated farm, a young Afro-American pulled a knife on Kenny. He reacted with such violence, that the man was hurled against an upturned cultivator. The man died instantly, a sharp prong piercing his heart.

That night Kenny drove down to the docks and was able to get quick work on board an Italian cargo boat. After a slow trip across the Atlantic, he jumped ship when the vessel docked at the port of Naples. Kenny found it easy to merge with the sleazy underbelly of the Italian docklands, where savage violence was often an everyday occurrence.

The two men sitting at the bar got talking and soon discovered they had much in common. By daybreak and after several rounds of beer, they had hatched a plan for a partnership. Having both hit rock bottom, it seemed now they had only one way to go …

They met up at the same bar the following afternoon and sat quietly alongside each other, both deep in thought.

Eventually Kenny ordered another round.

'Do you still think we could team up Paul, or do you think we were just two drunks dreaming up stupid fantasies? I mean, you're an educated man, my friend.' He chuckled. 'But I could wipe you out anytime if I felt like it, you smart-arse!'

'That's rubbish, Kenny. You had enough brains to slip away and then find your way to Naples. We will both need our brawn and especially our brains if we team up to make our fortunes.'

'I'm game, Paul; I guess we've nothing to lose anyway.'

'Well there are many openings for gentlemen of our persuasion here in Naples: robbery, prostitution, the protection racket, kidnapping for ransom... Take your pick.'

'Yea that's a good start. But they've all been overdone; we need to find something new.'

They were both silent for a while.

'What about selling religion?' Paul piped up.

Kenny laughed, 'Yeah I can just see us knocking on doors bible-thumping.'

'I didn't mean that, Kenny. I mean we could start a new religion — something different; we would attract a small number of wealthy business people who crave excitement in their lives, excitement of the violent variety. A secret society of like-minded top executives who were into dangerous sex games, and who'd be secure in the knowledge that their extra-curricular activities were undetectable. These kinds of guys pay top dollar to have tough discipline imposed on them. They thrive on decadent cruelty and pain and will pay us some serious money for the privilege.'

Paul gave Kenny a few moments to let his words sink in. Kenny seemed a little disturbed.

'That's quite far out, man. But it sounds like a good idea. How can you possibly get into that sort of thing? We'd need money we don't have to start a business like that. And how do we go about finding all these wealthy clients?'

Kenny waited until Paul returned from the outside toilet. Paul signalled the barman to bring more drinks.

'When I was in London I was introduced to that game,' Paul confided, pausing to look around the bar. Satisfied, he continued.

'We used to meet at an isolated cottage in Dorset. It was good at first, very engaging, but because of poor leadership, the whole thing gradually got out of hand. Discipline became lax. They should never have kept the same venue for their meetings.'

Paul emptied his glass and ordered another round. 'In the end a girl got killed and that night the cops moved in.'

'When you run this sort of club, you see,' Paul continued, 'you have to be extremely harsh on your clients, because that is just what they want. And instead of staying in the same place, you have to move around: a different international location for every meeting. There are a few men in London who would jump at the chance of joining us, and I'm sure they would have contacts in the USA and so on.'

'And what about the money?' Kenny asked. Paul laughed.

'We should demand a reasonable sum paid upfront to start with and then as these guys get themselves caught up in the net, we can gradually increase the fees. We should always demand payment in cash; it's safer and easier for everyone.'

Paul grabbed Kenny's shoulder and led him outside to the bar's back yard.

'Okay Kenny, let's just see how tough we are. Because if we're not, this scheme will never work.'

Kenny struck the first blow hitting Paul in the stomach, quickly followed by a blow to his chin. Paul immediately hit back with a fist pounding Kenny's collarbone and a kick to his left shin.

The next quarter of an hour they spent in brutal combat. Each time one of them fell to his knees, the other punched and kicked his opponent until he got up and it all started again. In the end, both men, exhausted and bloodied, sat alongside each other on the back step of the building.

'I enjoyed that,' spluttered Kenny, trying to speak over painful bouts of breath. 'I would call that a draw. That is the first time I have met someone who can put up as good a fight as me; we will make a bloody good team. No one will ever get the better of us, I reckon.'

'I was holding back,' spat Paul, hawking a gob of blood onto the floor. 'See, I really want you as a business partner, Kenny.'

'Like hell, you held back! I could have killed you at the blink of an eye. But I think you're onto a good plan here. So let's get started, buddy.'

★

It was just starting to rain as Paul, walking quickly up Oxford Street, turned off down a narrow lane. At the far end of the alley, he descended the five stone steps to arrive at the studded door of the Chalmers Club.

He pressed the doorbell and after a while a face appeared at the small eye-level grill. Paul stared right back at the face behind the grill and smiled. The door opened and Nigel the door attendant relieved him of his wet overcoat.

'Good evening Mr Paul, sir. Haven't seen you for a long time; I thought the AIDS had finally got you.'

'Hi Nigel, you are still a cheeky little bugger, aren't you? I must say I did go and get myself tested after I spent that night with you.' Paul laughed.

'The chance would have been a fine thing, sir. Go on

through Mr Paul: there's a straight-looking bloke waiting at the bar for you. He doesn't look too happy.'

Kenny slid off the barstool as Paul approached the bar.

'A large whisky, Kenny. It's good to see you, my friend.'

Kenny looked angry. 'Look, man: I don't care about your sexual preferences, but don't go involving me in this trash. I didn't realise we were meeting at a gay club.'

'Not to worry, old sport; I'll protect you from losing your virginity.' Paul held up his whisky glass. 'Cheers Kenny! We'll move over to that corner table as soon as our first potential client arrives.' Paul knocked back his drink and ordered another round.

'I'm guessing this client is gay as well. I used to bash gays when I was young. I could not stand the dirty little buggers. So you just watch your step, Paul, or I'll wipe you out too.' They both laughed but Paul knew that it was no idle threat from Kenny; he would have to keep his preferences under control.

At that moment a slightly overweight man in his mid-fifties, with greying, recently-cut hair, walked into the bar. Dressed in a dark blue pinstriped suit with a salmon-coloured tie, he took his place on the barstool next to Paul.

Kenny shivered when he saw the man: he reminded him of the judge he had once faced in court – the kind of man that would have no compunction in handing out a life-term or a death sentence even if matters had not been settled beyond reasonable doubt.

The man put his arms around Paul and gave him what Kenny thought was a much too intimate hug.

'I thought you would be alone, Paul,' he whispered. 'Who is this unsavoury character you've brought along with you?'

Paul laughed. 'This is my partner, Kenny. He'll be taking

care of our security, and other more unpleasant things. You can trust him with your life, Charles; but try to flirt with him and he'll kill you.' Still laughing he turned to Kenny.

'Kenny, meet Charles Sandman, a lawyer. He is the best protector of all the worst criminals in London,' he explained, adding, 'and, of course, the most expensive.'

'So just hope we will never need him; and if we do, that we would have plenty of money to pay him. Let's move over to that corner table, shall we?'

Paul signalled the barman to bring them a bottle of champagne and three glasses. 'You can hand the chit to Charles here.'

As they sat down, Charles pulled his chair up close to Paul.

'Hands on the table, Charles; we have business to discuss,' Paul chuckled, 'you old retrograde.'

'Paul, what's all this nonsense about forming a religious group? You know we tried this once before with disastrous results. Three of our members are still in prison and I just got away in the nick of time.'

'This would only be a cover for our real intentions,' said Paul. 'A false trail for the police. Our real clients would not be at all involved in that nonsense.'

'So? Tell me more,' Charles grunted.

His eyes fixed on Charles, Paul spoke slowly and quietly.

'Occasionally in some of your most serious and expensive court cases, Charles, you are faced with a witness for the prosecution who you know is about to destroy your client's defence.' Paul noticed a flash of interest on Charles's face.

'Then fate takes a hand. The poor witness has by chance met with a fatal accident. Oh dear, how tragic. But how fortuitous for your client. The case has to be dismissed!'

Paul continued. 'Then there is the top ranking businessperson who is about to clinch the deal of a lifetime; but there's just one person who is holding up the deal. Again, the poor man has a fatal accident.' Paul noticed the worried look on Charles's face and quickly continued.

'However, Charles, execution would be the very last resort. There are other ways to silent difficult people and that is where we come in.'

'A one off meeting with the 'target' would result in he or she being persuaded to fall into line. There are many methods: by blackmail, temporary kidnapping, the harming of a loved one or of course there is always the fear of physical torture.'

Charles leaned back in his chair and stared hard at both men.

'You are prepared to do all that? What if the witness decided not to co-operate?'

'Then the witness goes missing. That's the last resort. That's our worry and definitely not yours.'

Both Paul and Kenny laughed. Kenny watched Charles's face, his expression whose expression was a mixture of fear and greed. 'This is nothing new to us, old man. We can, and have, undertaken all these things before; so don't you ever think of doublecrossing me and Paul.'

Paul cut in: 'We have to persuade our victim nicely, or with pressure, to attend a meeting. These meetings are one-offs for each person. And we never hold two meetings at the same venue. This is the most difficult part: first we research their movements and then accidently bump into them when they are on their own and no one else is around. At gun or knifepoint we force them into our van and drive them to a deserted meeting place. The rest is easy.'

'The victim, Kenny and I, will be the only ones present and after the "softening up" process, we decide on the most appropriate action to permanently silence the person. We will not take on anyone with a criminal record, terrorists, politicians, police or public servants as they are more than likely already under police surveillance or protection.'

Charles had quietly moved his chair further away from Kenny and looked decidedly uncomfortable.

He turned to Paul.

'You have changed a lot since our previous encounter, Paul. As much as I would like to occasionally use your – I mean, both your services,' he grinned, 'I think your plans are extreme and highly dangerous and I would certainly not want to be involved in this hazardous enterprise.'

Paul leaned across the table took hold of Charles's hands and stared into his eyes. 'Charles dear, that's the last thing we want. The meetings just consist of Kenny, the victim and me. All we want from you is the name and a few details of the person that is causing you grief, and how much it is worth to you to be rid of him or her.'

Charles relaxed a little. Paul knew well that physical contact always had an immediate calming effect where Charles was concerned.

'Of course, Charles, it could be of great financial benefit both to you and your clients. If you were able to pass on these jobs to us, you know you would be well rewarded by your own clients.' Paul allowed his words to sink in.

Charles was quietly weighing up the possibilities. He knew several of his clients would welcome the idea and would pay a lot of money for this service.

'It could work. It could be very profitable. I do have the sort of clients who would welcome this type of service.'

Charles was smiling. 'In fact, Paul, if you can guarantee success without any involvement on my part, I might have something for you. Call me in the morning.'

Kenny stood up. 'I guess that wraps it up, guys. Come around to my place in the morning, Paul. We need to talk about this.'

Charles and Paul stayed seated and watched as Kenny left the bar.

'I don't like that fellow,' said Charles after some thought. 'He looks like the lowest type of scum that I have frequently had to deal with.'

'Kenny's all right; he's tough and vicious, but I'm pretty sure I can trust him and of course you know you can trust me. But just remember, my friend, I know enough about your nasty habits to finish your career at the bar.'

Charles slid his hand under the table and held onto Paul. 'And you know how much I have always felt for you, my boy.'

Paul helped Charles up. 'Come on Charles; your place or mine?'

Kenny's mind was going over the meeting he'd had with Paul and Charles. 'Bloody perverts,' he thought as he walked back to his apartment, only a little way past Tower Bridge. It was raining but it was only a light drizzle which Kenny hardly noticed.

He passed through Trafalgar Square and down Northumberland Avenue to the Embankment and then strolled along the banks of the Thames, which were quiet at this time of night, except for the call of an occasional seabird floating across the dark water.

Kenny suddenly heard a pair of hushed footsteps behind him. As he reached an unlit part of the walkway close to the overhead bridge, a couple of burly young men caught up with him. They grabbed hold of his arms, one on each side.

As if he was brushing off a couple of irritating flies, Kenny pushed his arms downward, freeing himself; then swinging them back up to shoulder height, he grabbed both men by their collars and brought their heads together with a sickening thud. Without hesitation, he dragged the two stunned youths to the river wall and heaved them onto the top of the wall.

Before they had time to realise what was happening, Kenny gently pushed them over the wall and into the water that was running fast up the river. After the resounding splashes, Kenny heard the startled cries of the adolescents fade off into the distance.

Kenny turned back, walked up Temple Avenue to Tudor Street and hailed a taxi to take him the rest of the way home.

★

It was just past 11.00 am and a bright sunny morning when Paul finally arrived at Kenny's flat.

'What kept you, Paul? I am not bloody waiting in all day for you. I have other better things to do like beating up that Jamaican dude that lives next door to me.'

'And like going to the pub and getting pissed, no doubt,' Paul chuckled. 'Sorry old boy, I had to catch up on some sleep. Anyway I have some good news for you: we have our first assignment. I have a name and all the necessary details. It's a pity we have to start off with such an attractive young woman.'

'That sounds interesting. Is it a local job?' asked Kenny. 'I don't care if she's Brigitte Bardot, so long as the money's good. What's it worth?'

Paul spread himself out on the leather sofa; Kenny handed him a beer and sat back in one of the armchairs.

'A man called Carl Bresnac is currently on trial for robbery and a vicious street murder. There was one person who witnessed the attack and she was able to pick him out of the line-up. Her evidence will have him locked up.'

'Charles has spent time with Carl and has been given all the details by the police. The incident took place near Russell Square and just outside the house of one rather attractive Sophie Dunalle, who saw the whole thing from her living room window. She's the witness.'

Paul finished his beer and Kenny passed him another.

'Sophie was able to pick Carl Bresnac out of a line-up; he was then arrested and charged with robbery and murder.'

'The police then found out that Carl was a recently recruited member of the East-end Contelisimo gang, a bunch of London boys involved in robbery and extortion. They also run a protection racket.'

'So Kenny, my boy', Paul continued, 'our newfound friend Charles, who has been called to defend his client, Carl, sent one of his go-betweens to approach the Louie Contelisimo gang, to see how much they valued Carl, and if they were prepared to pay a substantial fee for the removal of the only witness of the murder.'

'As it turns out, Carl Bresnac is also the son-in-law of Louie Contelisimo and Louie is prepared to pay a high price to save Carl. And I expect that's from being under a lot of pressure from his daughter.'

'So Charles has negotiated a deal with Louie for fifty thousand pounds – twenty thousand for himself and thirty thousand pounds for us, which is not a bad start for our business.'

Kenny walked over to the fridge and took out two cans of beer. 'Sounds good, but how are we going to eliminate this witness?' He opened one of the cans with a hiss and drank half of it in one go. 'And anyway,' he continued 'why would Louie want us to do this job, when he's got his own gang to do all his dirty work?'

'It's too close to home, Kenny. Louie doesn't want police attention: he knows they would turn his place over if it looked as though he had topped the girl. That's why we have to make it look like a convincing suicide, or just an unfortunate accident.'

'I don't think suicide will wash; the police would have detected any tendency she has to suicide. She seems a normal healthy young woman with a good job and a comfortable home.'

Kenny finished his beer. 'If the girl is smart and healthy, that won't make it easy for us to stage an accident.'

'She doesn't drive; she doesn't go swimming; we would be sure to miss if we dropped a brick from a construction site,' Paul laughed. 'That just leaves fire and unless we knocked her out first, I'm sure she would manage to escape from the fire.'

Kenny grinned. 'I could give her a push into an oncoming underground train, Paul.'

'She would probably drag you down with her.' Paul laughed again. 'Anyway you might have to wait a long time for her to be in the right position at the right moment.'

Kenny thought for a moment and then his face lit up. 'How about a hit and run? The girl, Sophie, right, must surely walk to a tube station every day. So why not organise a hit and run accident? It might take a few days to catch her crossing the road on her own, but after hitting her, I'm sure I could make a clean getaway and dump the car somewhere where you could wait to pick me up.'

Paul was silent for a while, considering the idea. 'That's not a bad idea, Kenny. Of course we would have to leave the country immediately after the accident. Since we flew into England in a chartered aircraft no questions asked, we should leave the same way – no passports in and no passports out – easy.' He paused, 'I will give my friend a call and see if he is available to help. He will have to be prepared to stand by for the next few days, as we can only do the job if Sophie is on her own when she crosses the street.'

'We would need to pay a premium to have the aircraft on standby for a few days while we waited to finish the job,' Kenny said. 'And we'll need to hire three cars: a heavy four-wheel-drive to do the job, your car to pick me up and a third car ready to do a switch just in case I am seen getting into your car.'

Paul leaned back in the armchair. 'We can easily afford all that. We should move out of our flats and into a small hotel now; our apartments were paid for in cash, so providing we carefully clean and remove any evidence of ourselves from the apartments, the police won't even know we have been living in England.'

'So where do we go once we get to France?' Kenny asked.

'Italy,' Paul replied. 'I think a nice little cottage in Tuscany would make a good base for our future operations.'

At exactly 8:30 am the next day, the two men stood in the light rain and watched Sophie come out of the apartment block; she was wearing a scarf and a dark red raincoat. She walked briskly in the direction of South Kensington Station, just two streets away. The two men followed discretely keeping a safe distance behind her.

About a hundred yards down the street, a quiet

residential road with no traffic, Sophie crossed over using the traffic lights at the pedestrian crossing. She turned left and then right into the next street before crossing over again at the traffic lights, where she disappeared into the Underground Station.

The two men walked back to the first street. 'I think I'll park on the other side of the road facing this crossing,' Kenny said, eyeing the length of the road from the parking spot to the traffic lights. 'You'll wait for me over there with your engine running. As she steps off the pavement to cross the road, I will slowly move forward and then hit her at full throttle when she is halfway across.'

Paul nodded. 'That sounds about right. Let's walk around to the next street and see where we can abandon your car.'

They walked to the next corner to find a similar residential street. A short way down, there was a passageway that led over to a parallel street.

'Perfect,' said Kenny. 'You park near the top of this narrow lane, after killing the girl I will abandon my car and run up the lane jump into your car, where you will be waiting. We'll be away before anyone realises what's happened. We can drive to the car park at Sainsbury's – that's about a mile away – and change again into the third car. Then off to Essex.'

'You know if you don't kill her, Kenny, you will have to finish her off with your gun. She has to die or we don't get paid.'

Kenny snapped back. 'You do your job; I'll see that she dies quickly. Trust me: she won't know what hit her.'

'Okay, Kenny, I trust you, mate. I'm sure you'll make a good job of it. Next up, we'll check out the hire cars and make sure the four-wheel drive has a bull bar; that'll really finish her off. I've got the aircraft organised and waiting, starting to tomorrow.'

'So it's all set for the morning.' Kenny smiled.

Paul took a deep breath. 'Yes, mate, it's all settled. I'll see you at the Hotel Pleasant tonight.'

The two men went their separate ways.

★

Later that evening Paul met Charles in the Chalmers Club.

'It's all organised, Charles darling. Tomorrow morning at around eight thirty, young Sophie will be coming out of her home and we will be waiting in the next street. If all goes according to plan, by nine thirty, you'll be able to call on your client and collect the money.'

Paul described the details of their plan to kill the girl and make their escape using the aircraft to take them across to a landing strip on a farm in a quiet part of Normandy.

Charles walked over to the bar and returned to their table with a bottle of champagne and two glasses.

'You boys certainly don't waste time. As you will not be around to celebrate the success of this your first job, you and I will have to celebrate tonight and thankfully without your partner, Kenny. He scares me, Paul.'

Paul laughed. 'Dear Charles, Kenny is no worse than you and I; only difference is that he finds it impossible to keep his feelings under control. Cheers.' He drained his glass, which Charles quickly refilled.

'Do you remember that farm you took me to once in Suffolk; it was near Orford? We would like you to meet us there at between four and five tomorrow afternoon with the cash. Make absolutely sure you are not followed as it is possible the police will be watching you.'

'That's a long drive, Paul; it will be closer to five or six before I can get there.'

Paul gripped Charles's wrist. 'I said, between four and five. Understand? And if you don't turn up, we will come and get you. I will leave your punishment in the hands of Kenny, God help you.'

CHAPTER 4

Sophie awoke with a start. She had overslept having worked late into the night on a case that was due to start in the Crown Court in two days' time.

She leaped out of bed discarding her nightgown and headed for the shower. She decided to wash her hair, even if it made her a little late in getting to her office; she didn't mind being just a little bit late for a meeting with one of her most unpleasant, but also most important clients.

Her mind wandered back to her mother, Jackie, as often happened when she washed her hair. Sophie's earliest memories were playing on the beach at Dee Why on Sydney's North Shore. Jackie and her father Sam were both keen surfers and spent a good deal of their time on the beach with their surf boards.

When Sophie was six months old, they took her down to the beach and set up a small tent close to the Surf Club. Eager friends were always there to look after Sophie while her parents were out riding the waves.

Those first six years were very happy days for Sophie, running wild with all the other children on the beach, then lying resting with her mother and father in their Igloo tent, sheltered from the burning sun.

Sadly, the idyllic days of her childhood came to an end a few weeks after her sixth birthday. It was a day like any other: bathing in the bright afternoon sunshine and making up nursery rhymes with her mother, Sophie's ears suddenly became filled with the sound of the lifeguard's whistles.

Jackie stood up; she could see what was happening in the surf and she dashed screaming down the beach to the water's edge. She began to wade out and then just froze, horrified at what she was seeing.

Two lifeguards were dashing out through the surf towards a man who was being attacked by a large white shark. Jackie stood up to her thighs in the water, watching the spectacle of blood mixing with white foam just a few metres ahead of her. Were it not for her daughter, she would have plunged into the water to pull Sam out with her bare hands, but as it was, all she could do was to wait for the lifeguards to return with what remained of her husband.

In the commotion that followed, Jackie's best friend, Connie, picked up Sophie and rushed off the beach and carried her to the ice cream shop. A few minutes later, a surfer from the club came up to them and spoke quietly to Connie. Sophie, unaware of what was going on, was happy to go back to Connie's house to see her two Persian cats.

All Sophie knew was that her father had disappeared: the waves had taken him, and for many months after the incident she would lie in bed with her arms wrapped around her crying mother.

In the months that followed Sam's death, Jackie slowly woke up to the reality of her life as a single mother. Sophie was similar to Sam in so many ways that she often felt that he was there with them.

Sam had inherited quite a large sum of money from his parents, which Sam had passed on to Jackie. So Sophie's mum was left comfortably off and had no need to ever have to work again. Sophie profited from a childhood spent with a devoted mother, who was determined to give Sophie a good education that finally enabled her to study at Oxford University in England, where she decided to study law.

Soon after she left Australia, her mother was diagnosed with an aggressive form of lung cancer. She died six months later, and Sophie returned home to be with her for her final few weeks.

Sophie returned to Oxford three months later an orphan. She had decided to leave Australia for good, having sold her mother's house, tied up all legal affairs and said goodbye to all her friends. All she had when she arrived back in England, were two suitcases of her most precious possessions.

She dealt with her grief and feelings of emptiness by burying herself in her work. Sophie was determined to become a solicitor, knowing that it had been her mother's wish, and indeed, qualified three years later.

★

Sophie finished washing her hair and moved over to the window where she had left her hair dryer. She stood there looking out of the window whilst she dried her hair.

Sophie was tall and slim, with the typical Australian long blond hair and lovely smooth olive skin. She was a girl with character, enthusiastic, creative, compassionate, but strong when necessary, and always with a happy disposition when in the company of others.

She was still wincing from the dressing down, which she had received at the police station the day before. She realised how stupid she had been in literally running away from the scene of the crime after having witnessed, from the window of her apartment, the girl being attacked and knocked to the ground by her attacker. She had clearly seen the face of the girl's attacker and should have reported it to the police.

Instead she had slipped out of the building and then taken the Channel tunnel train to Paris where she later met up with her friends.

Definitely not a good start to her first job as a solicitor, all because she didn't want to miss the holiday in France with her old university friends.

As she watched the people crossing the road at the traffic lights, she noticed a girl wearing a red raincoat, just like the one she usually wore. Two children were running up behind the girl, when suddenly to her horror, a large four-wheel drive car headed straight towards them. At the very last second the car braked, coming to a halt just inches from the girl and the two children.

The children kept running and disappeared down the street. The girl stood still, just staring at the driver.

Sophie heard two sharp cracks. The girl collapsed onto the road and lay still. Then the car, with tyres screaming, shot down the road and disappeared around the first corner, having completely ignored the red traffic lights.

Still staring in disbelief at the murder scene, she noticed another man getting into his car and driving off. Sophie thought she recognised this man as Charles Maidham, a solicitor she had recently seen at the police station, who was defending Carl Bresnac, the killer of the first girl that she had seen murdered.

Sophie reached for the telephone, dialed 999 and calmly, as she had been told in no uncertain terms by the police officer the day before, described in detail exactly what had happened to this second murdered girl. She did not mention seeing the solicitor as he had been further down the street at the time and she was not certain that it was him.

This time she was the calm and competent solicitor and was thanked by the duty officer.

Sophie found it hard to believe that she had now actually witnessed the death of two girls in her street.

By the time she reached the scene, the girl's body was being loaded into the ambulance.

★

'You know this was meant for you.' The detective who had interviewed her the day before came and stood beside her.

'So why wasn't I protected? Do you realise the poor girl was wearing a red raincoat just like mine?' She grabbed his arm. 'This girl would not have died if you had been doing your job properly.'

'Yes, miss. It was brought to our attention that the man you identified is a member of the Contelisimo gang and they really are a very nasty gang of crooks. If you don't mind I would like you to come back with me to the station. With your help, we might be able to nail these bastards. From now on we will be keeping a watch in case they try again.'

At the police station Sophie called her office and asked someone to cancel her appointment. Again she carefully described exactly what she had seen from her bedroom window.

As she was already a witness in the Carl Bresnac murder case she decided not to mention the fact that she might have seen Charles Maidham getting into his car after the murder in the same street. She realised that as she was not entirely sure it was Charles she had seen – if it was not him – it could make all her evidence in court less plausible to the jury.

After an hour of discussion, having put all the information and facts together, they realised that there was nothing they could do until they were able to prove that the Contelisimo gang was behind this second murder.

★

Two months later, Carl Bresnac was found guilty of murdering the first girl and was sentenced to life imprisonment.

It was at his trial, being viciously interviewed by Charles Maidham in court, that Sophie knew for sure that he was the man she had seen getting into his car and driving away, on the day the girl in the red coat had been shot.

Sophie decided to keep this to herself until she was able to talk to him. It might just have been a coincidence that he'd happened to be there at the time, but she was pretty sure that since he was representing Carl, he must be somehow involved in the killing.

As it happened, unknown to Sophie, although undeserved, Charles received five thousand pounds from the Contelismo gang. As for Kenny and Paul, they got nothing as they had killed the wrong girl. They were lucky to escape to France in the light aircraft. They decided to lie low in Paris and now being short of money, had to wait in the hope that Charles might come up with another job for them in the near future.

Charles was wise enough to realise that Kenny and Paul, because of a red coat, had just been unlucky in killing the wrong girl; otherwise, they had been most professional in the way they'd handled the murder.

★

As hard as she tried, Sophie could not let the matter rest. Although she was satisfied with Carl Bresnac's trial and sentence, she found the police follow-up of the second murder frustratingly slow. After all, it was supposed to

73

be her that was killed that day and it was just through an unlucky chance, for the other girl, who was wearing a red coat, that she Sophie was still alive to tell the tale.

So Sophie decided she would personally track down the man who'd murdered the girl in the red raincoat. That bastard had to be around somewhere, and she was determined to find him. Moreover, she was convinced that the solicitor Charles was somehow involved in all of this.

After carefully considering her options, she decided to call on Charles. Sophie took the Underground train to Bank Station; then walked to Leaden Hall Street. She turned off into a narrow lane and entered the dingy offices where Charles operated his doubtful business. A surly-looking man, who looked more like a minder than a receptionist, was standing behind the reception desk.

'Watcher want? Charles don't want to be disturbed so go away.'

Shocked by his response, Sophie pushed past him to the door, which was obviously Charles's office and gently opened the door a little. There were five men seated around the long boardroom table, two of them were Asians and the other two looked like Russians, or Eastern Europeans. Charles had his back to her. She quickly withdrew and closed the door.

Sophie realised she had interrupted an important meeting but she needed to talk to Charles when he was alone. She tried to push the man aside, as he tried to block her way out. 'He's gonna fly-away overseas tonight so don't ya come back again.' He growled at her as she finally managed to slip past him and out into the street.

Sophie returned to her office and methodically called every airline, until she finally found that Charles was booked on a flight to Paris at seven thirty the following evening. She also discovered that Charles had booked himself a First Class ticket on a flight, from Paris to Sydney, Australia, a few days later.

On the spur of the moment Sophie decided to book herself on the same flights in Economy Class where she could follow his movements without being noticed by him.

Sophie realised that her anger for Charles and his associates was taking over her life, which made her even more determined to find out what Charles and his friends were about to do. Even if it was not connected to that unfortunate girl's murder outside of her house, she was still determined to destroy Charles; she felt so sure he must have been involved in the killing.

As money was not a problem for Sophie, she decided to go all the way to Sydney and further if necessary to nail these bastards. She felt excited at the prospect of going back to her beloved Australia. Sophie stepped across the passage to the senior partner's office to ask him if she could take the following month off, to visit some friends in Sydney.

'Sophie darling,' he drawled, a pained expression on his face. He quite fancied Sophie but was actually happily married with three young children. 'You have only just started working here. However since you are not yet too involved with any of our clients, it is probably the best time for you to get away for a few weeks.' He slipped his arm around her waist; Sophie removed his hand as it slid down her back towards her bottom.

'Just go for it whilst you can, dear girl.' He smiled. 'Of course you won't get paid any holiday salary,' he added.

CHAPTER 5

'Who was that woman, Charles?' Karl Grunsteig demanded.

Karl Grunsteig – originally from Russia – was the leader of an extremely powerful gang of international criminals, known in Eastern Europe as the dreaded 'Swordfish Gang'.

Born into the mire of Soviet communism, Karl grew up watching the system, and his country, collapse. His family was connected to a faction of the South Russian Mafia and Karl quickly rose to the top of his chosen profession as an international criminal; a ruthless and cruel associate to all that crossed his path. Torture and murder had always been the tools of his trade, and he now lived in London in a secluded warehouse conversion overlooking the Thames.

At the same time, Karl was a family man. He loved his wife, Louise, with a passion and was devoted to his two children, a boy of nine and a six-year-old daughter. His family was the main reason he had moved to London from Moscow, as he wanted both his children to be educated at an English public school.

To the outside world, Karl was just a London businessman with a normal happy family. Even his wife Louise knew little of the darker side of his exploits.

His family in Russia, who had strong connections with a certain Middle Eastern terrorist organisation to whom they supplied arms from Russia, had originally been instrumental in bringing Karl to meet Charles. They also had access to an old Second World War Russian submarine that was about to become very useful to him.

Karl had decided to use the services of Charles, who in the past had proved himself to be excellent at organising and running operations. Charles had contacts with the best criminals in London, but more than that he had an intense fear of Karl, and would do anything he wanted.

Karl enjoyed the power he had over Charles's weaknesses, though he always ensured that Charles was well rewarded after a successful operation. Karl was happy to use Charles to do these jobs for him, thus divorcing himself from any direct connection to any dirty work.

The previous year, Karl had taken his family to Australia for a three-month holiday. Driving up north from Sydney to Brisbane, they stopped off along the way to see the small towns of Hawks Nest and Tea Gardens from where they took a boat trip up the Myall River to the Great Lakes. Karl was so impressed with the natural beauty of the area that, after talking to the locals, he decided to go to Bulahdelah and hire a houseboat for three weeks.

They had a wonderful holiday exploring all the many hidden backwaters of the lakes. Then one warm evening, towards the end of their third week, when the children were asleep in their bunks and Karl and Louise were quietly sitting on the deck of the houseboat, Karl noticed a movement in the bushes. They were docked in a tiny backwater surrounded by tall reeds and paperbark trees that hung perilously over the still water. Karl blinked for a second and then looked back into the bushes. He thought what he saw looked like a person, but it might have been an animal.

Most people would have dismissed that sort of sighting, but Karl's instinct drove him to investigate further.

He slipped his all-purpose hunting knife, the knife that he had used on many an occasion to kill or injure his enemies, into his belt and quietly slid into the water.

Louise poured herself another glass of champagne and leaned back in her deckchair. 'Boys' games again,' she sighed.

During his short tenure in the Russian Army, Karl spent time with an old tracker from East Africa, who had been hired by the Russian Army to train its troops on how to track down terrorists in difficult terrain. Karl learned many skills which later proved very useful to him in the course of his criminal activities.

He waded quietly up to the bank of the lake and then silently disappeared into the bushes. Realising there were snakes about, he withdrew his knife and headed up to where he had seen the figure.

Karl waited patiently for several minutes. The slight sound of a branch breaking alerted him. As he slowly moved forward, he heard another sound of rustling leaves as if someone or something were moving through them. Whatever it was, it was moving very slowly. Karl followed, keeping his distance. He wanted to see where this creature was going. He noticed then that they were climbing a fairly steep slope.

The sounds stopped. Karl came to a clearing just a few yards wide, on the far side of which there was a large banksia bush. He noticed a gap at the bottom of the bush. Knife in hand, Karl suddenly threw himself into the hole in the bush.

As he stood up, he was amazed to see that he was actually at what seemed to be the entrance of a cave. There was a loud screech and what appeared to be a man with a beard, long straggly hair and dressed in animal skins, rushed past him and disappeared into the bush. Shocked, Karl came out into the clearing, but the man was gone and Karl knew now he would never find him.

Karl went back to look inside the cave. There was a thick layer of rubbish covering the floor and the rotting remains of uneaten food. A dead animal lay on large stones ready to be cooked on the smoldering fire. A pile of skins, which he guessed was the old man's wardrobe, lay close to the back wall. The creature's bed was close to the fire, which looked as though it had been recently lit. It threw a light which cast strange shadows across the cave walls making the whole scene seem so unreal.

As his eyes became accustomed to the light inside the cave, Karl soon realised, to his astonishment, that he had entered by a partially open heavy steel door, the sort used in wartime fortifications and bunkers. It was then that he also noticed the steel boxes stacked against the back wall.

He went across and lifted the lid of one of the cases.

'My God. It's a cache of guns and ammunition. This must be a left-over from the Second World War.'

Karl tried to pick up one of the cases. As he lifted the heavy box, the bottom gave way and what he thought was ammunition spilled all over the floor.

Cursing, he sank to his knees and began picking up the bits of metal that were scattered all around him. They were smooth and rectangular and a very strange shape for bullets. Unless …

Karl held one of the pieces up to the firelight and it reflected back a warm yellow glow. His heart missed a beat.

Gold! He was kneeling alone in a cave in the Australian outback surrounded by five cases of gold bullion that were worth a fortune beyond his wildest dreams.

His mind began to race. How did the gold end up here? And who was that strange man? He looked like something from the Stone Age. Karl guessed that he must have been guarding the gold and the people that had left him there had either died or had forgotten him.

A little shaken at the luck that had brought him to this enormous fortune, Karl wandered back through the bush and down to the houseboat, deep in thought. Somehow he had to get all that gold out of Australia and back to Europe. But how?

He decided it was better to leave the old man to guard the fortune until he was ready to come back. Ideas began to flood into his super-active mind.

'Did you find anything, darling?'

'No. It was probably a dingo wandering through the bush.' Karl tried hard to tame the excitement in his voice.

He poured himself a glass of champagne and was careful not to let Louise see that his hand was shaking.

'This holiday in Australia has been a really interesting and exciting experience, but I think it's time to return to London now, sweetheart.'

Shortly after dawn the next morning whilst his family slept on, Karl carefully drew a map of the area and marked in roughly the position of the cave. He smiled as he concealed it in his briefcase, still excited at this remarkable find.

He was tempted to return to the cave, but decided the less he disturbed the undergrowth there, the better. It had remained hidden for over fifty years so should be safe for another year or so. He would come back to collect the gold when he completed a plan to get it safely out of Australia.

★

'What woman?' Charles looked surprised.

'She opened the door and looked at us sitting around the table and then she quickly backed out and closed the door again.'

Seeing the concerned look on Karl's face, Charles became scared. Karl was a dangerous and ruthless man to whom Charles felt inextricably tied. He tried to laugh off his anxiety but ...

'Must have been some stupid woman urgently wanting a divorce,' he said in a casual tone. 'She will probably make it up with her husband tonight.' His attempt at humour was wasted on Karl.

'Well we have finished our meeting now, Charles. Arrange for your two men to report to our agent in Brest as soon as possible. From there, he will help them to be taken out by launch to the passing Russian freighter. You realise, of course, they cannot be allowed to enter Australia legally,' he added.

'Eventually, that old Russian submarine that we chartered will meet up with our freighter, forty kilometres north of Newcastle in New South Wales, on the eastern coast of Australia. Your men and all the necessary equipment for the operation will be transferred from the freighter to the submarine. If all goes well, two days later they will set off from the submarine in a large inflatable close to Broughton Island. This is a small deserted isle just a few miles from the coastal beach where they will land and where you will meet them.'

'I'll meet them on the beach with the truck and trailer,' Charles interjected.

'You then just transport them and the inflatable a short distance up a sandy track, cross a deserted road, and you'll find yourself in a camping site, where you can re-launch the inflatable into the Myall Lakes.' Karl looked thoughtful for a moment.

'We will give your men one week to find and to re-pack the gold. They must have it ready for when I give the order to transfer the inflatable and the gold to the beach and then straight out to the waiting submarine.' Karl got up and stood behind Charles, putting one hand on his shoulder and curling the fingers of the other hand gently around Charles' neck. Charles winced.

'Now Charles, tell me exactly what it is you have to do.'

Charles, chilled from the sensation of Karl's fingers on his neck, stuttered slightly. 'I, um, fly to Paris where I will brief my two men. I will then take them down to Brest and deliver them to your agent in Brest. Then I get a flight from Paris to Sydney, where I will hire a large four-wheel-drive truck and a trailer able to carry a five-metre inflatable launch.'

Karl cut in. 'It might be better to buy one, Charles. You have the money and you can sell it after we have finished the operation; that would draw less attention to us. Continue, Charles.'

'I then drive it up to a small village called Bulahdelah and park the truck and the trailer in a garage where it won't be noticed.'

Karl slapped Charles lightly on the cheek. 'You will have to organise that before you buy the truck and trailer, you idiot. Understand? Good. Now go on, Charles,' he murmured.

'I will then go to the boat hire people in Bulahdelah and purchase one of their houseboats. That's a big outlay, no? Then I will spend the next few days with the houseboat, finding my way around the lakes and will look for that place where you discovered the bunker.'

'You can re-sell the houseboat when we have finished the operation and we are well away from Australia. I think you'll also need to buy a light motorcycle to keep on the houseboat,' Karl interjected.

'Yes, I know. I will also need a small dingy to bring the motorcycle from the shore to the houseboat. I will then moor the houseboat near the Weldon camping site, use the bike to get back to Bulahdelah, then take the truck down to the Denham Park Hotel in Newcastle and wait for your telephone call. You said it would be about six weeks after leaving Paris for Australia, right?' Charles started to sweat.

In response, Karl tightened his grip around Charles' neck.

'Please, Karl …You're hurting me,' Charles whined.

'That gives you plenty of time, Charles, so I expect you to have everything ready for us by then. That's good, Charles; I'm sure you will fully execute your part of this enterprise. Carry on.'

Karl let go of Charles's neck and Charles gently massaged it back to life and wiped away his tears. He continued, 'When I have been informed of the arrival time of your inflatable launch at the ocean beach – which will be close to the Weldon camping site – I will drive the vehicle and the trailer to the beach, using the access track which is close to the camping site and will meet up with my two men on the beach.

'We will load the inflatable launch and stores on to the trailer and then drive to the camping site. From there, we will re-launch the inflatable into the lake and motor out to the houseboat with all the supplies.'

'Good boy Charles.' Karl gave Charles a much harder slap across the face. 'And then?'

'As an extra precaution, because there is not too much cover to hide the houseboat at the backwater where the bunker is, we will have to take the houseboat to that hidden backwater you told me about a little way from Nerong, which I'm sure by then I will have found.'

'The following day, after fully briefing Paul and Kenny, I will take them on a short tour of the lakes with the launch and then on to the small backwater where the bunker is hidden. After making sure that they know exactly what they have to do, they will take me back to the camping site.'

'Slow down, Charles, I am finding it hard to understand you. I realise you are shit scared of me; but that's not a bad thing.'

'Paul or Kenny will take me back to the camping site. I will drop the trailer off at the Bulahdelah garage, then drive back to the Denham Park Hotel, park the truck somewhere close by and wait for your call a few days later. I will be there at the hotel until the job is finished, or in case I am needed if things go *awry*.'

Karl gave Charles one last slap. He took great pleasure in tormenting this homosexual wimp.

'They had better not go awry, Charles. In my world, failure will be a painful death sentence for all three of you. You must keep in touch with them at all times. Mobile phones don't always work there so you might have to pay them a visit, but that means hiring another boat so be very careful not to draw attention to yourself or the two of them.'

The other men in the room stood up. They were ready to go.

'And when do I get my share, Karl? I will need a lot of

money when I get to Australia.' Charles almost whimpered as the Russian towered over him. Not many people scared Charles, but Karl really did.

'You will get fifty per cent now, paid into an account in Hong Kong. This will be more than enough to cover all the necessary expenses, the rest of your share will be paid three months after the completion of the job.

'When the time is right, Charles, you will transport the gold out to Broughton Island. I will come with the submarine to collect it from there. Your men will come back with me, but you will have to stay on to tidy things up and cover-up all our tracks.'

Maybe, Karl smiled to himself. He had in fact already decided that Charles, Paul and Kenny were too great a risk and would have to be eliminated as soon as the job was completed.

CHAPTER 6

Having received the long-awaited call from Karl, Charles was now on his way to meet up with Paul and Kenny. They had landed on the ocean beach 18 kilometres north of Hawk's Nest.

Charles was now fully aware that Sophie was following him and he had decided that it was time, with the aid of Paul and Kenny, to finally get rid of her.

His phone rang. It was Paul to say that he and Kenny had arrived three hours earlier than originally planned and were waiting on the beach with the inflatable loaded with all the necessary supplies.

Their arrival at the beach had been relatively easy; the submarine had surfaced the previous evening at dusk and their large inflatable had been launched and loaded with all the necessary supplies. They had then set off with an experienced sailor, who was also a radio operator and headed for Broughton Island, a deserted island just a short distance from the Australian coast.

After pointing out the exact landing spot on the distant beach to Paul, Greg, the wireless operator, carried his equipment on to the island where he was to set up his transmitter and would liaise between the submarine and the shore party. He watched as the inflatable headed for the exact spot on that endless beach before setting up his camp and sending a message back to the submarine.

★

Charles was excited as he realised it gave him an ideal opportunity to use the two men to get rid of the bloody Sophie girl.

'Look,' he said to Paul, 'if there are no other people on the beach, I want you and Kenny to take the track that runs up from the beach to the main road. When you get there, you will see a small car park. If no one's about, wait for me there but make sure you keep out of sight until I arrive. Let me know if you see anyone there.'

'I am being followed by a girl in a car. It's Sophie, the one we failed to kill in London; this time, we really have to finish the job. You understand? Call me when you get to that car park and hurry as I'm not too far away.'

'Will do, Charles,' Paul replied. 'There is no one about on this beach and the tide is going out so the launch will be safe to leave for a while. Kenny will be happy to have some action. We are on our way.'

Charles smiled. Sophie was the girl that they had failed to kill. She was also the girl who had stood up in court to testify against his client. Charles was not bothered at losing that case – the man was a nasty piece of work and deserved what he got – but he was angry at losing his £30,000 retainer.

He realised Sophie must have seen the girl that Kenny had mistaken for her, murdered. Kenny had attempted to mow down the girl in the red raincoat but failed as two children got in the way. He then had to kill the girl that he thought was Sophie with his gun. A most unfortunate mistake Charles mused. Especially for the unfortunate girl.

Charles realised that Sophie must have spotted him getting into his car that day.

Going there to watch the murder had been a mistake on his part. Now he was implicated and Sophie was again a witness. There really was no other alternative than to have Sophie killed.

Things had become very complicated. His client had robbed and murdered a girl. Sophie witnessed the murder, so he'd arranged to kill her as she was the sole witness. Then his hired man went and killed the wrong girl, and again Sophie was the sole witness from her bedroom window. So now they had to murder Sophie, and the murders were just piling up.

Charles had not noticed Sophie on the plane coming out to Australia; she had changed her appearance, having dyed her hair (normally blond, but she had darkened it), removed all her makeup, worn some dark glasses and dressed in a plain black trouser suit, hoping Charles would not notice her following him.

It was at the hotel in Sydney that Charles first noticed Sophie; she had followed him into reception. He was getting into the lift with his luggage to go to his room when he saw her checking in and realised the same woman had been following him through customs, immigration and on the train to the Sydney hotel. He realised it must have been the same girl that had poked her head into his office the day he met with Karl and his associates. Somehow she must have found out that he was travelling to Sydney and had been following him since he landed in Australia.

To follow him across the world, Charles decided, Sophie must have a death wish, or else she was just plain stupid. He was quite confident that this time, if he could lead her into the car park, Paul and Kenny would have no problem in killing her. It would be easy to get rid of her body somewhere in the vast unoccupied part of the lakes and State Forest.

He drove down the hill through the small town of Tea

Gardens and then over the Singing Bridge to Hawk's Nest. He turned left on to the deserted lakeside road, which ended at Bombah where the ferry crossed the lakes.

To continue on from there, he had to cross the lake by ferry to Myall Shores and then follow a long winding road to Bulahdelah in order to join the main Sydney highway. Charles noticed an Aboriginal girl standing on the corner thumbing a lift. He ignored her and drove on.

Paul called him to say that he and Kenny had arrived at the car park and that the place was deserted.

He advised Charles to take his truck to the far end of the car park and then switch his lights off and turn around to face the way he had come in. He and Kenny would stay out of sight close to the entrance to the car park.

Paul told Charles, 'As soon as she comes into the car park, drive forward, blind her with your headlights and ram her car. Leave the rest to us.'

'That sounds good but don't kill her yet, Paul. We need to find out if she is working alone, and how much she knows about our plans; we will have to force her to talk. We don't know if she is alone in Australia or working with the police. She could easily be leading us into a trap. But I'm sure Kenny will know how to make her talk.' Thinking about Kenny, Charles almost felt sorry for the girl.

Sophie, following Charles from a little way behind, also saw the girl waving, thought she might be in trouble and stopped.

'Can ya give me a lift, darl? Me boyfriend is camping at Bombah and its miles from here.'

'No problem, my dear; jump in.'

Sophie noticed the girl was tall, slim and quite beautiful.

She had long black hair and features that made Sophie think maybe that sometime in the past she had a white ancestor.

'Thanks love. Me boyfriend is camping there and ya know, the bastard left me stranded at the pub in Tea Gardens.'

'Tell me when to stop and I'll drop you off.' Sophie was a little annoyed at herself for stopping for the girl, as she had now lost sight of Charles.

'Sure, darl. Me mates call me Fran but I'm really Frances. It's quite a long way down this road ya know.'

★

Charles, realising that Sophie was now a long way behind, waited in the road until her car came into sight. Then, when he felt sure she had seen him, he turned into the car park. Paul waved from the trees as he drove past to the far end of the lot, where he turned around ready to face the entrance.

★

After driving about twenty kilometres down the road, Sophie suddenly spotted Charles's truck and trailer, turning to the right. Sophie slowed down. At the same time Fran yelled. 'Don't turn off here, darl; it's much further down the road.'

Sophie was getting tired after the long drive from Newcastle. She ignored Fran and, throwing caution to the wind, drove into the unlit car park.

She was surprised to see Charles's truck facing her. She suddenly realised it was coming straight towards her, with its headlights full-on.

The four-wheel-drive struck her car sending it sideways for a few metres. Both braced themselves in the silence, stunned by the shock of the impact.

Suddenly the front doors were flung open and the two screaming girls were dragged out of the car by the two men, who then forced them to lie face-down on the rough track. Kenny leaned over each girl holding his favorite killing knife at each one of their throats. 'Shut your trap or I'll slit ya bloody throat,' he hissed

Charles appeared with some rope and his first-aid box. Within minutes both girls were securely trussed up and Paul using large Band-Aids, reinforced with bandages, ensured their silence.

'We've got two for the price of one,' Kenny laughed.

Paul stared down at the two bound and gagged girls. 'I don't know who the dark one is, but now we will have to get rid of both of them.'

'I saw that dark girl thumbing a lift; I'm sure she is not involved,' Charles said. He was excited. 'So now we have two girls to kill. The Sophie girl should have died in London, but that time you botched it up. She has followed me all the way over to Australia.' He bent down to speak to Sophie. 'But now, Sophie girl, you have finally walked into our trap, haven't you?'

Sophie looked up at this ugly revolting pervert. As he got closer, she desperately wanted to spit in his repulsive leering face.

He straightened up furious as he noticed the other two men were laughing. 'That's thanks to me, chaps, we now have her here. So you know what to do now, Kenny,' he sneered. 'First you must make her talk! Do your worst! And then we silence her forever.'

'We can't do anything now, Charles. We must go down to the beach and collect the boat before any of the local fishermen arrive.' Kenny picked up Sophie and carried her over to the truck, dumping her on the back seat. Paul carried Fran over and dropped her next to Sophie and then climbed in beside them.

'Come on, let's go. It will be getting light in just a few hours from now.' The other two jumped into the wagon. Charles, who had many years' experience driving on beaches, took the wheel, whilst Kenny sat silently beside him. They drove along the trail leading down to the beach.

The tide had dropped; the large inflatable launch was high up on the sand so they had no difficulty winching it up on to the trailer. They reloaded some of the supplies they had taken out of the launch in order to lighten it so that they could drag it well clear of the surf when they landed.

That done, they set off back to the launching ramp at the camping site. This was a little way further down the road on the opposite side to the car park; the distance from the ocean to the lake was less than one mile.

They were able to re-launch the inflatable into the lake without unloading all their gear. The two girls, who were fully conscious but securely gagged, were carried out and bundled into the launch. Charles then quietly steered the launch out to the houseboat.

After transferring all the supplies and equipment to the houseboat, Charles decided to tow the launch behind the houseboat and move over to another of the small hidden lakes that Karl had discovered during his family holiday. It was on the Nerong side of the Bombah Broadwater but not anywhere near the bunker. They would go to that place later when they were quite sure they would not be seen.

'The girls can stay in the launch until we get to this quiet backwater; then you can deal with them.' Charles' deviant mind was getting more excited. He was looking forward to watching Paul and Kenny torturing the girls before killing them.

'Don't worry, Charles; we will make it very stimulating

for you.' Paul, knowing all about Charles's sexual perversions, knew how to get him really excited.

★

Sophie and Fran lay close together facing one another in the bottom of the launch. They were both wide awake and very much aware of their predicament.

Fran was smiling; she had been in situations like this when she was a child, living in the bush with her family. She had been tied up and tormented and beaten by the boys when she was only twelve years old. After this experience Fran had spent many hours learning how to untie knots and free herself, in case one day the boys came back to molest her again.

Within minutes her hands were free; she removed her gag and then untied her legs. She leaned over and whispered into Sophie's ear.

'I'm gonna free you, darl, but don't make a sound. Can ya swim? Nod ya head.' Sophie nodded.

'Okay. 'Cause we goin' fast, darl. The front of the boat is up but I can see over the back end. Lookin' over the back end I know where we is. We is going away from Tamboi, the entrance to Myall River that goes right down to Tea Gardens. It's goin' to be a bloody long swim.'

Fran untied Sophie and removed her gag. Sophie carefully massaged her previously tightly tied legs to bring them back to life.

'Now darl, we are getting father and father away from Tamboi so we have to get out quick. They must not see us slip out of the boat into the water. Keep still and low in the water and don't start swimming until the boat is gone out of sight. Follow me, darl.'

Sophie watched as Fran silently slid over the transom

of the launch into the dark water without making a splash. Sophie quickly followed. They watched as the houseboat and the launch disappeared into the darkness.

The lake was shallow and the water was warm. The girls exchanged smiles of relief at their escape and started their long swim to Tamboi. Sophie gave Fran's arm a squeeze under the water.

'Thanks darl.'

★

The houseboat and launch had almost reached the other side of the lake. Kenny, sitting in the main cabin knocking back his third can of beer, was wondering how best to kill the two girls. He was looking forward to a little sadistic fun with them first.

He realised Paul and Charles would enjoy watching him make Sophie talk. He got up and went rummaging in his kitbag, found his cigarette lighter, pincers and cut-throat razor, Kenny slipped them into his pocket. He knew he could very quickly make the girl talk, but that would spoil his fun. He would take his time and the three of them could enjoy watching the girls suffer before he finally killed them. There would be no mistakes this time.

Kenny went to the stern rail of the houseboat and leaned over to look at the girls.

'Shit! The buggers have gone!' He screamed and ran back to where Charles was steering the houseboat.

'Stop the boat, Charles!' he yelled.

Paul came running up to the stern. 'I've got the flash lamp. Pull the bloody launch alongside, Kenny, and jump in. They can't have got far. They will still be swimming in the lake.'

'Wait for me.' Charles ran to join them, not wanting it miss out on their recapture.

'Stay there, you bloody idiot; someone has to guide us back to the houseboat.' Paul leaped into the launch grabbed the tiller and the outboard motor roared into life.

'Let go the rope, Charles; we won't be long.' Paul was not so sure they would find them. It was a large lake and dark; the girls could be anywhere by now.

They sped back the way they had come, but Paul soon realised in the darkness that he had no idea which way it was. There was some light in the sky from the bright stars and in the distance he could see a very faint outline of the land. Straight ahead he guessed was the river entrance which Charles had pointed out as they motored past it on their way across the lake. He would head in that direction.

Kenny sat in the bow of the launch scanning the water ahead as they sped towards Tamboi, the river entrance. He felt the razor in his pocket. He would show no mercy this time. He would kill the dark one immediately and also the Sophie girl if she gave him any trouble.

Charles was leaning on the rail of the houseboat, sick with fear. He knew that if the girls got away, that could be the end of their mission and Karl would surely kill him. Charles leaned over the rail and was violently sick. He moved back to the cabin, washed his face and poured himself a large whisky. His hands were shaking and half the whisky spilled on the floor. He sat in one of the armchairs, cursing himself for getting into this mess.

★

Fran knew exactly where they were. She had been fishing for prawns and swimming in the lake for most of her life. She knew that if they could reach Tamboi, they would climb up the river bank and could easily disappear into the thick bush area. No Whiteman could find an Aborigine in that bushland and even though she had some white blood, she was still at heart an Aborigine.

Sophie was a little way ahead of Fran and as she turned to see where she was, to her horror she saw the white bow wave of the launch coming towards them. She tried to yell but swallowed some water and started to cough. Ahead Sophie could see some rocks and tall rushes a little way outside of the river entrance. She realised they could not reach the river in time; the launch was speeding straight towards them. If they could reach the rocks, they might not be spotted by these men.

Sophie headed for the rocks cutting her feet on the wild oyster shells as she scrambled over them to the patch of reeds. She turned and yelled to Fran to come and join her.

Fran ignored her and carried on swimming, sure that she could reach the river bank in time.

Sophie lowered her body into the water, hidden by the reeds but still able to watch with horror; she knew Fran must have been spotted. She heard the boat's motor roar as it raced towards Fran. She watched as Fran turned to look at the boat racing towards her.

Then she gave Sophie a little wave, turned towards the river mouth and continued to slowly swim towards it. Sophie knew at that moment, Fran was deliberately giving up her life to save her from the men in the boat.

Fran saw that she had no chance of reaching the river bank and knew that she was about to die. She would not turn; they would not see her fear or her tears. She would die with dignity as she had been told to, so many times by her elders.

Sophie heard the thud as Fran was struck on the head by the sharp bow of the launch. She stifled a scream and watched the launch as it did a full circle until it got back to where Fran's body floated on the water.

They hauled Fran's body onto the launch. Sophie fought back her anger; tears streamed down her face and into the muddy water where she crouched. 'I will get those evil bastards,' she sobbed. 'I will tear them limb from limb. They will pay with their blood for this.'

Sophie watched as the boat slowly circled the area and then went back out into the lake to look for her; she stayed where she was, not daring to move.

Still searching for her, the boat turned around and headed for the reeds where she was hiding. Sophie took a deep breath and, holding on to the reeds, pulled herself under the water until her lungs felt they were about to burst. Then she allowed her face to come to the surface, took another deep breath, and submerged again.

When Sophie finally raised her head above the water, the launch had turned away. She watched as they headed for the river mouth and waited until they were out of sight and she could no longer hear the motor.

Sophie slithered out from among the reeds into the deep water and started to swim to the river bank about two hundred metres away. She finally scrambled up to shore, ran through a patch of the long grass, and collapsed amongst the thick bushes and trees that covered that area. Sophie had no thoughts at that time for the many snakes that lived in that part of the bush.

She was alive. Fran was dead.

★

'I think I can see something dead-ahead, Paul!' Kenny yelled.

'I've got it.' Paul gave the motor full throttle, the launch leaped forward towards the swimmer.

Kenny searched the water for the second swimmer but there was no sign of her. He pushed Paul aside and took over the steering, heading straight towards where he'd seen the figure. 'I don't know which one this is but she sure ain't gonna survive this time,' he yelled.

There was a distinct thud as the sharp bow struck the girl, splitting her skull open and killing her instantly.

Paul looked on horrified. 'At least that was a quick death for her. She was a brave girl, Kenny; she never looked back.'

Kenny had a nasty smile on his face. 'I enjoyed that. Especially as it was the black girl. But she got off too lightly. When we find the other girl she won't be so lucky.'

'We have to find her first, you maniac. Let's pull this one on board and then make a circle around this area. If she's not here then we will start looking down the river. It will be light soon.' Paul took over the steering and brought the launch alongside the still floating body.

They heaved her on board, laid her body on the floor of the launch and then headed out onto the lake again.

They made several circles to the left and then to the right. They went outside of the entrance and then headed back to the river. Kenny shone the torch on the patch of reeds where Sophie was concealed, but luckily for her, at that moment her head was under the water.

'It's down the river now, Kenny. We'll go down slowly. Shine your torch on the river banks; we might just see if there are any marks where someone might have scrambled up to the shore.'

They went slowly down the river, past a row of huts

and sheds, the motor just ticking over, not wanting to draw attention to themselves in case there were any fishermen about.

'We won't find her now Kenny. We might as well continue down this river until we find a good spot to get rid of the body.'

Kenny grunted. His warped mind was thinking about the body and what he was going to do with it.

Swinging his torch form one side of the river to the other he spotted what looked like a small island surrounded by reeds.

'Just take the launch up that creek, Paul; I think that should do.'

'Okay, put the nose of the launch in as close as you can. I'll get in the water, pass me the body and back away. And leave me here for a few minutes whilst I sort things.' Kenny whispered excitedly.

'Don't be too long Kenny; it will get light soon and there are bound to be some fishing boats about.'

Paul took the launch across the river and, once around a slight bend, he was able to slip in amongst the tall reeds, well out of sight of any passing boat.

Kenny dragged Fran's body onto the tiny grass-covered island. He could see it was just starting to get light. As soon as Paul was out of sight, he slowly undressed Fran's body, his hands shaking with excitement as he stared at her dark skin and smiled. 'Not an American girl.' He murmured, 'but still a darkie.' A sudden thought went through his warped mind: in the past, sometimes when he had killed someone, he had left behind his trademark to satisfy his ego.

He took out his sharp knife and cut off one of Fran's hands, wrapped it in her underwear and slipped it into his pocket. This would be a nice surprise for Charles and proof that at least one of the girls was dead. Kenny dragged the body to the shallow water behind the island. He placed several large stones on top of the body; then satisfied that it was well out of sight he waded back to the island.

It was now daylight. Paul saw Kenny waving. As there was no one in sight in either direction, he brought the launch across to the island. Kenny waded out to meet him and climbed aboard the launch.

They had not eaten since earlier the previous day; they decided to take a chance and head back to the houseboat. They motored back up the river and passed a group of huts along the shore.

'Looks like we missed these huts in the dark,' Paul said. 'There is no one about and they all look empty. We had better take a look in case the Sophie girl got as far as here. She could be hiding in one of these huts.'

Paul brought the launch alongside a rickety old jetty. The two men ran between all the cottages and looked inside. All were empty except for one which they noticed had a recently broken window. It looked to them as if someone had recently tried to break in. They smashed the front door and searched the cottage for any signs that showed the girl had entered through the broken window.

'No sign of the Sophie girl here,' said Kenny. 'Usually these birds leave some sort of mess behind them.'

Paul laughed. 'What would you know about these sorts of girls, Kenny? Your types usually live in brothels.' He dodged the blow from Kenny. 'I'm sure she wouldn't have made it this far so let's get moving before any other boats arrive.'

A short time later they steered out of the river and into

the Broadwater. They passed the area where they had killed the girl and headed for the houseboat.

'Keep a lookout for Sophie's body in case she was a poor swimmer and just drowned. It could be floating around here,' Paul yelled.

'Don't talk crap, Paul. She'd be lying on the bottom somewhere.

Let's get back, I'm starving.'

CHAPTER 7

It was still early when Paul and Kenny returned to the houseboat to find Charles had worked himself into such a state, that he was near to collapse. It took several large whiskies to calm him down.

After some discussion, they decided that the Sophie girl must have drowned and they hoped that her body would now be lying somewhere at the bottom of the lake. However, if it did float up and was later found, there should be no marks on her to suggest she had been attacked.

Charles regained his composure after his third whisky and was now satisfied that Paul and Kenny had taken care of the two girls. To celebrate, he decided to cook them all a large breakfast.

'When you chaps have finished this lot we will take the launch as far as Nerong and back,' he bellowed over the noise of eggs frying on the gas stove. 'It will be less noticeable to the locals than taking the houseboat. After that, I'll give you a quick tour of the lakes in the launch before taking you to the bunker where you'll be working.'

Kenny was staring into the bush. 'Guys, I think we are being watched. There is someone standing close to that large paperbark tree by the edge of the water.'

'What the hell is that?' murmured Charles. 'He looks more like an animal than a man. We had better get rid of him. Who wants to go after him?'

'Leave it to me, guys.' Kenny quietly moved out of sight to

the back of the houseboat, slipped into the water, and swam in a circle, keeping well out of sight of the old man.

Kenny carefully worked his way through the reeds until he came out close to where the strange creature was still standing. It was an old man, dressed in animal skins, and he was standing, frozen, staring across at the houseboat. It was as if he was confused and didn't know what to do.

The truth was his brain was addled. Back in 1942, he had received a terrible beating when he had been caught stealing supplies from a party of American Navy personnel who had been sent to explore a potential training area. In absolute terror he managed to escape his captors and disappear into the bushland that surrounded the lakes, but the incident had left him permanently brain damaged.

During the long years that followed, he had managed to survive by living off the fruits and edible vegetation that grew in that part of the bush. The animals that he was able to catch and kill provided him with meat and the protein that he badly needed. The skins from these animals kept him warm throughout winter months.

Ever since his escape that terrible day, he had always lived in fear of all human beings. Then one day his life in the bush took a turn. He had been stalking a wallaby, following it along a narrow track that led into tall thick bushes. He lost sight of the animal, but as he moved further into the thick undergrowth, he found himself facing a large heavy steel door. He managed to open it and once inside discovered the concealed cave.

At last he had found himself a shelter. The cave was to be his secret home for many years to come.

He saw there was a stack of cases in the cave, but presumed they belonged to the human people who had terrorised him. His frightened, addled brain refused to go touch the cases, or even go near them. He always kept his distance: sitting on the other side of the cave, where at night he would light a fire. He instinctively knew to always make sure the flames were extinguished by daybreak in case anyone might see the smoke coming from the bushes.

After decades surviving in the bush, the man had grown old. He was frail now and his feet and legs were badly swollen, as were his throat and tongue. His breathing had now become very difficult; he was in great pain and he could no longer feed himself. He knew his time was almost up, and now, with nothing to lose in his twilight years, he found himself mysteriously drawn to other humans again.

While he stood staring at the houseboat, he was actually debating whether to surrender himself to the people there. Perhaps it was time to leave his jungle home; perhaps these people could help him?

But the old man's thoughts were interrupted with a start as Kenny jumped out in front of him.

His immediate reaction was to turn and run away. He started to run but soon found his tired legs were giving away. The man chasing him was very close behind and the old man let out a frightened screech as Kenny caught up and grabbed his long hair. The old man was so terrified that he didn't feel the pain as Kenny's knife struck him in the back. Death was a welcome relief to this strange old man.

Kenny dragged the old man's body into a thick bush and covered it with leaves. He felt quite elated as he strolled back to the water's edge and swam out to the houseboat.

'No problem. All sorted. Get me a beer, Charles, and I'd like another plate of bacon and eggs, please,' he grinned.

'You cold-hearted bastard, Kenny,' Paul laughed.

Charles remained silent and just handed Kenny a beer.

Minutes later, they emerged from the backwater and Charles guided the launch out towards Nerong Harbour.

The three men glided into Nerong Harbour, which appeared to be deserted. Though it was no longer early, there was still a chill in the air. Two empty cars were parked near the harbour jetty. They stopped to admire the houses and boats in this tucked away part of the lake.

Kenny slipped his hand in his pocket and felt something cold and damp.

'Charles, I forgot; I had a present for you.' He handed Charles the bloodstained underwear.

Charles slowly unwrapped the severed hand. 'Oh my God! You wicked evil bastard.' He immediately flung the hand into the water and watched it sink to the bottom of the harbour.

Paul put a restraining hand on Kenny. 'I think we should be moving on now. Just calm down, Charles; at least you have proof that one girl is dead.'

Charles realised he must get away from these two men as quickly as possible. During their first few hours here on the lakes they had already killed three people. He knew it had to be done and he got a certain amount of pleasure watching Kenny and Paul inflict pain on their unfortunate victims. But even his warped mind was unsettled by the way Kenny could so calmly murder and mutilate.

'Look chaps, I am going to show you where the cave is, where you will be doing this job for Karl. Then you can drop me off at the camping site. I have to move the truck and trailer away from there as the police will no doubt soon be looking for the two girls.'

The launch slipped quietly out of Nerong Harbour

but then sped across the lake to the place where Karl had discovered the bunker. Charles decided to skip the tour of the lakes, as he was now impatient to move the truck and trailer.

He carefully navigated the launch into the concealed creek, following the marks that Karl had noted when he was last there. The launch was now no longer visible from the lake, but to make absolutely sure, Charles edged the vessel through the tall reeds that surrounded the creek.

'How do we find this bunker, Charles? And then what do we do? Can we put a few bars of gold aside for ourselves?' Kenny leered.

Charles shot him a withering glare. 'Are you insane? You know you left Karl on the submarine near Broughton Island. He's most likely come ashore by now and will be monitoring every move we make. But you can be sure he'll be doing it from a safe distance.' Charles shuddered at the thought.

'Charles is right, Ken,' said Paul. 'There's too much at stake to mess around. If Karl catches us robbing the till, he'll go ballistic. He'll surely kill the three of us. And it won't be a nice death.' Paul realised that, for once, they were completely outclassed by this mastermind criminal.

Paul was also concerned about the outcome of this whole enterprise. Once the gold was on the submarine, he believed it more than possible Karl would want to eliminate the three of them.

'Anyway chaps, here is a sketch map that will lead you to the bunker.' Charles produced a crumpled sheet of paper. 'Your job is to transfer all the gold bars into those secure bags and then into the nets. Then place them back in the cases until it is time to take them to the beach; all the bags and nets are in that box by your feet, Kenny.'

Charles lowered his voice, his fear of Karl now overtaken by his greed for some of the gold.

'I've been thinking chaps; Karl never said how many bars of gold were there. When I looked at the gold myself, I could see that only the top cases had been opened. There are several underneath that haven't been touched.'

Kenny cut in. 'Well, what are we waiting for? We should take some for insurance in case Karl cheats us.'

'Guys, if Karl finds out we have robbed him, only God will be able to help us.' Paul was beginning to get nervous about the idea of stealing from Karl.

'Look, Karl might not have counted the bars of gold, and I'm sure he won't have counted the bags and the nets. You can take twelve nuggets of gold in three bags down to the water and submerge them in a place that can only be detected by us three. I will show you exactly where you can drop them into the lake.' Charles paused to give Kenny the time he needed to absorb the instructions.

'Okay, I'll go along with this,' Paul added thoughtfully, 'but if Karl discovers we have cheated him it will be curtains for us. We cannot touch that gold until a long time after this job has been completed.' Paul paused. 'We might even have to wait years before retrieving those bars.'

They followed Charles and waded out into the water until they were almost shoulder high and about twenty yards from the shore. The sandy bottom was covered by a thick layer of seaweed which made it difficult to see anything on the lakebed. Charles pointed out two large trees that stood next to each other on one side of the curved line of the creek and two more that stood on the other side.

'When those four trees are lined up chaps, where the two imaginary lines cross; this is where the gold will be. So

107

Paul, you wade up to those two trees on the left and carefully mark them with a knife and Kenny wade over to the two on the right. I will wait here to make sure you mark the right trees. So now, chaps, we will all remember exactly where our gold bars are.'

Charles' voice returned to its normal pitch. 'So, when you have finished packing all the gold bullion, get ready to transfer it to the beach. We will wait for a departure time from Karl and when it comes I will call you and tell you to bring the gold over to the camping site. I will be waiting there with the trailer to take the gold – and the two of you of course – to the beach, before you head for Broughton Island and then out to the submarine.'

'There should be a large piece of cake ready for us when the job's done and another piece waiting here at a later date,' said Kenny, with an uncharacteristic smile.

'All sounds so easy, Charles. Let's hope it is.' Paul had his reservations. 'You realise we will have to sell that gold in Australia. That won't be easy.'

'There will always be a good market for gold, especially among the rich Asians who live in Australia,' Charles replied. 'It might take time to sell it all, but we can live like kings in the meantime. Drop me off at the camping site now, will you, Paul? I think you guys should get back to the houseboat. Tomorrow, bring your gear over to this place well before daylight. Make sure you conceal the launch amongst these reeds. When you are ready, you can go up to the bunker on that hillside and start work. Wait until it gets dark before you start your journey back to the houseboat.

'And where are you going, Charles?' Kenny demanded.

'I'm going to a nice comfortable bed in Newcastle.'

'And leave us to do all the work, you lazy bastard!' Paul

laughed. 'Maybe we will stash your share of the gold where you can't find it.'

'Do that, Paul, and I will just tell Karl you have cheated him. He really will skin you alive.'

★

Sophie was exhausted after her long swim. Despite the deluge of emotion she had experienced, watching Fran being murdered and herself narrowly escaping those evil monsters, she still managed to drift off to sleep. She awoke a few hours later to find it was starting to get light and that it would soon be sunrise. She was cold and stiff as her half-naked body had been lying in the long wet grass for several hours. As she slowly and painfully dragged herself to her feet, all the events of the previous night came flooding back to her.

'Those evil bastards,' she muttered. 'They murdered that poor girl in cold blood and I just watched it happen. But what could I have done? If I had shown myself I would be dead as well.' Sophie was consumed with anger and frustration at the night's events.

She straightened up and looked around. She was standing on the end of a narrow peninsula which jutted out into the lake. Further out on the water, she saw the rocks and reeds, which she had managed to reach before the men had spotted her, and where she had been able to hide herself under the water amongst the reeds.

The peninsula was covered in thick long grass and dotted with the occasional casuarinas or paperbarks. She could see that there were a lot more trees further down the river and what seemed like the roof of a house in the distance.

Looking down at her feet, she saw they were badly scratched as were her hands. This had happened whilst scrambling over the rocks to the shelter of the tall reeds.

She had lost her shoes when casting off her clothes before starting that long swim and now Sophie was only wearing her pants and a light t-shirt.

At least it's not cold she thought but wondered what she would do when she met up with other people.

Sophie walked cautiously through the long grass, keeping a keen eye out for snakes as she headed towards the trees and undergrowth further downriver.

The house she had spotted in the distance turned out to be an old shack with a rusty tin roof; it was just a few yards from the riverbank. She then saw several other similar huts scattered along the river bank, but there was no sign of life around, and they all looked empty.

She wandered around, peering into the windows of the larger ones; they were just open sheds with a bed and basic cooking utensils.

Sophie found one, a cottage, which looked slightly better equipped than the rest. She guessed there might also be a few cans of food inside, and her stomach rumbled at the thought.

There was a padlock on the front door but none of the windows were open. She decided to break in, so picking up a heavy piece of wood she smashed the glass, reached inside, slipped the catch and was able to open the window wide enough to let herself in.

The house was pretty basic; the main room had just a table and chairs, several large cupboards and a double bed on one side of the room. It looked as if the owner had a wife or partner. A door led through to a fair-sized kitchen, with a screened shower at the far end. She opened a cupboard in the kitchen to find a jar of sugar, a salt shaker, a few damp tea bags, a bottle of tomato ketchup and a few rusty cans of beans. She let out a whoop of joy as she took a tin opener from the top drawer and cut one of the cans open. She emptied its juicy orange contents into a bowl and shovelled them into her mouth with a teaspoon.

Satisfied with her breakfast, Sophie went to the shower to see if the water was connected. She turned on the tap and to her delight was sprayed with a stream of lukewarm water. She stripped off and with the aid of a very suspect piece of soap, washed herself and her scanty clothes under the shower. Still dripping, she went and found a tatty old towel in one of the cupboards.

It occurred to Sophie that the men could still be searching for her. She realised she must be careful and be prepared for them to come back and search these cottages.

She quickly slipped on her wet clothes, unbolted the kitchen door that opened out at the back of the house and stepped out into the tall grass that surrounded all the houses.

There was a pile of old shoes just outside the kitchen door. She found a worn-out pair of thongs that almost fitted her and decided to explore the back area of the shacks in case she had to make a quick getaway and hide from the men.

Sophie soon realised it would be easy to hide in this rainforest area, amongst the banksias, blackbutts and cabbage tree palms. The bushes would make it very easy for her to conceal herself. Looking up at one of the swamp mahoganies she spotted a koala bear nestled on a top branch. She smiled and gave it a little wave.

Sophie returned to the cottage and carefully tidied up. If the men came back they would see no sign of her having been there. After wandering around the other huts and cottages she came back, got on the bed and within minutes was asleep.

Awakened by the sound of a motor, Sophie peered out of the window. She realised it was the same inflatable launch from the night before. As it came up the river, it started to slow down. They were coming to search the huts.

She quickly tidied the bed, carefully closed the window, and, grabbing the empty beans tin, slipped out closing the back door behind her and disappeared into the rainforest.

Well concealed inside a large bush, she heard the motor stop. Sophie held her breath and waited for what seemed like hours.

Then suddenly she heard the motor start again. She listened to it as it roared up the river, and waited until the sound gradually faded away into the distance.

Returning to the cottage, Sophie saw that the kitchen door was open. They had been in to search for her; she could smell their cigarette smoke.

She felt relieved and decided that it was now safe to stay there until perhaps someone else came by in another boat.

Finding a large piece of cardboard and some pens, Sophie wrote HELP in large letters and put the sign just inside the kitchen door.

In one of the other shacks, Sophie had found a fishing rod that used feathers instead of bait. She decided to go fishing off the river bank.

Sometime later, to her surprise, Sophie was rewarded with a nice-sized black fish; which she cooked outside on the homemade 'barbie' and ate with another rusty tin of beans. Then she made herself comfortable in the rickety old bed, having first carefully checked the sheets for spiders and other invading insects.

Sleep did not come easily to Sophie. All that fish and that rusty tin of beans had definitely not been a good idea.

She woke up at dawn the next day feeling like death. She staggered outside and was violently sick. Food poisoning had taken its toll. For the next six hours Sophie vomited and retched until she was completely empty and exhausted.

By late afternoon, having recovered enough to make herself a cup of tea, she went back to the bed and fell into a deep sleep from which she didn't wake up until early the following morning.

CHAPTER 8

Marçel glanced at his watch; it was six o'clock and a beautiful sunny morning. He showered and shaved on the boat's little bathroom before coming out on deck and closing his eyes to listen to the cacophony of birdcalls of the dozens species that flourished around the Great Lakes.

Having cooked himself a hot breakfast, Marçel settled down and carefully studied the charts and local maps of the lakes. Satisfied that he had a good idea of the layout of the waterways, he started the two powerful motors, untied the mooring ropes, climbed up onto the upper bridge and set the motors at 'slow ahead'. He gently eased the cruiser out into the river and headed down to the Bombah Broadwater.

It took him two hours travelling at a modest speed down the unspoilt peaceful river to reach the Broadwater. Though he had been told that there were no visible houses on the shores of the vast Bombah Broadwater, he still spotted two along the way.

Marçel crossed the Broadwater and decided to continue on down the Lower Myall River, past Tea Gardens, and then on to where the river finally ran into Port Stephens Harbour. He sped across the lake to the Lower Myall River entrance, an area called Tamboi.

A short distance down from the head of the river, on the right-hand bank, he saw what looked like a deserted collection of huts which were in fact occasionally used by the local fishermen. Seeing no sign of life there, Marçel continued, slowly making his way down towards Tea Gardens, which was more than fourteen miles down the river.

All the while, he was carefully scanning the riverbanks for any sign of a woman's clothing. He was praying he would not find a dead body.

It was lunch time when Marçel arrived at Tea Gardens. He tied the boat up to one of the jetties and strolled across to the hotel bar for a long cool beer. The owner was friendly and suggested he try their excellent prawn salad, which he did.

One hour later, Marçel reluctantly tore himself away and continued on to Port Stephens, passing a large area of oyster beds on the way down. He was surprised at the size of Port Stephens Harbour, later discovering that it was far larger even than Sydney Harbour.

He decided to return to the river, by-pass Tea Gardens and have another look for clues on his way back up to Tamboi. He circled around the beaches and small islands near the river exit before heading back up the river.

Because he was now heading upriver, he found he was looking at the banks from a different angle. It was in an area called Brass-Water that he noticed a small side-lake.

Marçel spotted something white floating in the water amongst some of the tall reeds. He took the boat into this shallow area, risking running aground. He edged the cruiser up to the reeds and then realised there was a small island hidden away amongst the foliage. With the boat hook he carefully lifted the white cloth out of the water and onto the deck of the cruiser.

He carefully reversed the boat away from the reeds and dropped the anchor in the middle of the river so he could pause to examine what he had pulled from the water. It was a white short-sleeved woman's blouse, and it was dotted with bloodstains. He looked for other clues on the piece of clothing, but all he found was a small label on the inside that read 'Made in China'.

Marçel immediately pulled out his mobile phone called Detective Sergeant Morrow. He explained where he was, and told him what he had found.

'Well done, Marçel. Can you get the blouse to me as quickly as possible? Try not to handle it as we will be sending it to the lab. If it hasn't been in the water too long we might be able to pick up something from a blood analysis. At least we know the blouse comes from China,' he sighed.

'I think there are some more clothes on a little island close to where I found the blouse but I didn't want to disturb anything till you got here. If you like, I can return to Tea Gardens and pick you up from there.'

'You say there are more clothes on an island?' The sergeant paused for a moment. 'Stay there. I am going to call the police boat to bring me down to where you are. This could be important. Do you have a dingy?'

'Yes. What do you want me to do?'

'Go in close and see exactly what's on the island, but don't land. I will need you to take me there in your dingy. I happen to be at Nerong at present and the police boat is not too far away from here. You can call me back and tell me exactly what you see there.'

Marçel rowed the dingy into the large area of reeds. He used an oar to pole the dingy through the tall grasses.

After forcing his way through the reeds, he came to the shore of the tiny island that was covered with lush green foliage. There were clothes scattered around the place and a good many footmarks. He decided to go back to the cruiser and call the detective.

'It's what I thought, Sam,' Marçel told him on the phone. 'There are clothes and footprints all over the tiny island.'

'I am on my way; should be with you in one hour's time.'

Exactly an hour later, the police boat arrived. Marçel rowed alongside and the detective climbed down into his dingy.

He steered the dingy back through the reeds until they reached the grass bank and scrambled up onto the island.

'Bingo!' cried the detective. 'Here they are. The woman's clothes are scattered around, as if she had undressed – or was forced to undress – in a hurry. We don't want to spoil all these footprints, Marçel.'

Sam used the camera on his mobile phone to take several photos of the scattered clothes and then slipped on some thin rubber gloves. He slowly picked up each item of clothing and after examining it carefully, put it into a small plastic bag, of which he had several stuffed in his pocket.

'I don't understand this,' Sam muttered under his breath. 'Except for the bloodstained blouse which you found in the water, it would appear she took off her clothes, or was forced to undress right here. But what happened then?' He paused for a moment.

'Over here, Sam!' Marçel called out across the island. 'There are some drag marks in the grass.'

'Bugger! Marcel, I think we are about to find the girl ...'

They found the body of the young Aboriginal girl in the shallow water amongst the reeds. It had been weighed down with several large stones, and her sightless face was just a few inches below the surface of the water.

Sam took a few more photos before they dragged her

117

body up onto the grass. The girl was naked and the back of her head had been split open. One of her hands was missing. They covered her with the blanket that Marçel had fetched from his boat. Sam called the station and requested a team be immediately sent to Tea Gardens to collect the body and search the area for more clues, and he dispatched the police boat to go and fetch them.

'You might as well get back to Bulahdelah now, Marçel. My team will be here shortly and I will have to stay around for some time to clean up this mess and see if we can find any more clues.'

'Well, at least that's one girl found Sam; let's hope the other one is still alive, but it's not looking too good is it? Poor girl; what a terrible way to go! There must have been more than one person involved in this murder, I reckon; evil bastards. We'll find them, won't we?'

With that Marçel turned towards his dinghy. 'I'll see you in the morning, Sam.'

'Try not to be around at Bulahdelah tomorrow morning,' Sam replied. 'I want to talk to the boat hire people. It's best if they don't know that you're connected to this police investigation.'

Marçel was surprised and somewhat disappointed. 'Sure Sam,' he replied. 'If that's what you prefer.'

Sam noticed Marçel's face. He looked like the wind had been knocked out of his sails.

'Look mate: the police launch is dropping me off at Nerong, where I parked my car. Why don't you tie up there tonight? That's if you wouldn't mind putting me up for the night…'

'Good idea! We could have a beer or three.'

'And we will bring your dingy back, Marçel, I promise.'

★

118

Once again, Sophie woke to the sound of a motor boat engine. She looked at her watch: it was past eleven in the morning. She jumped out of bed and peeped out of the window to see if the murderers were coming back to look for her.

Sophie was relieved to see a large motor cruiser coming down the river. She was beginning to worry that maybe nobody ever came this way and she would eventually starve to death. Anyway she smiled; mostly she wanted to get into some decent clothes.

She peered through the dirty window as it came into full view and noticed that there appeared to be only one person on board. He was a tall man, and even from a distance Sophie could tell he was exceptionally handsome. Her heart jumped a beat. Had she seen this man before? *In my dreams*, she thought; she certainly had no time in her current situation to be thinking about handsome men. Yet, she found she was still picturing the man even after the cruiser had passed the huts and headed down river.

'Shit. I should have run out and called for help,' she thought. 'The crooks just had a houseboat and an inflatable launch.' She dashed down to the river bank shouting and waving her arms as the cruiser disappeared around the bend in the river.

Deflated, Sophie wandered back to the cottage. It was too late now, though perhaps he might come back this way later, she thought.

Sophie tidied up the bed, took a cold shower and put on the scanty clothes that she had washed the previous evening. There was one very old towel that she managed to tie around her waist and wear as a skirt. If that dishy man on the cruiser came back later, at least she would be decent.

Feeling hungry, Sophie re-lit the fire, warmed up a can of beans and, despite her experience of the day before, looked for a non-rusted tin and then made sure the beans were very well cooked. She boiled some water and made a mug of suspect-looking tea. It occurred to her that she was putting herself in a vulnerable situation if the crooks were still looking for her; the smoke from the fire would be a dead giveaway.

She promptly threw water on the remains of the fire.

Sophie spent the rest of the day wandering around admiring the many trees and shrubs that were growing right down to the water's edge. There were so many different species, all competing for the limited space on the river bank.

It was late afternoon, whilst sitting on an old log at the back of the cottage, when she heard the motors again.

Without thinking, Sophie leaped up and dashed down to the riverbank. Standing behind a large tree trunk, she peered downstream listening to the approaching sound. When the boat appeared from around the bend in the river, to her relief and delight, it was the cruiser.

For the second time that day, Sophie's heart missed a beat.

She dashed back to the cottage, wrapped the old towel around her waist, grabbed the 'Help' board and ran back to the riverside.

It was the same man standing on the top deck steering the cruiser. Sophie felt really excited, and she knew it was not just at the thought of being rescued.

When Marçel saw the girl standing on the riverbank his heart also missed a beat; and it was not only because he had found the missing girl.

Unbeknown to both of them at that moment, fate had

brought Sophie and Marçel together and from now on their lives would be changed for ever.

Marçel brought the cruiser close to the riverbank. Sophie waded out the short distance and scrambled up the short ladder on the stern of the boat, losing her towel in the process.

Marcel beckoned her to come up to the bridge. Sophie tried to grab her lost towel before it floated too far away from her grasp. She blushed as she turned back around to face the handsome stranger. He put his hand out towards her and she climbed up to the bridge. Then not knowing what to say, she grabbed his outstretched hand and shook it vigorously.

Marçel, stunned by the girl's natural beauty just stared back at her and wondered if she could actually talk at all! He felt he knew her and yet they had never met. 'Are you … are you the missing English girl?' he stuttered.

Before Sophie had time to answer, Marçel realised they were bumping against the riverbank. He pushed the throttle forward and brought the cruiser out into the centre of the river.

'Yes. We can't stay here; they might come back any time. I'm being hunted down by some very dangerous, very evil men,' Sophie blurted hurriedly, reaching out to touch her rescuer's arm.

Her touch was like an electric shock to Marcel.

'Right,' he paused, feeling increasingly flustered. 'We will go up into the lake and then you can tell me exactly what happened to you and the other girl.' He decided it was not the appropriate time to tell her that the other girl was dead; far better to wait and let Sam break the bad news.

Marçel inspected Sophie from head to toe and then

laughed warmly. 'Go down below and help yourself to any of my clothes. You might find them a bit big for you, but I'm sure you will manage somehow.'

'Hey, what's your name?' he shouted as she descended the ladder.

'Sophie. What's yours?'

'Marçel!' he yelled.

'Nice name,' she murmured as she entered the main saloon.

Marçel gave the engines half throttle and they cruised up to the top of the river and out onto the lake. On the way up, he called Sam.

'You actually found her on the river bank at Tamboi? That is one hell of a relief, Marçel. What sort of condition is she in? Has she been injured? Do you think she might have been sexually assaulted?'

'I don't know, Sam, but I'm about to find that out. She was very scantily dressed when she waved for help, but she seems quite cheerful, all things considered.'

'I'm sure her lack of clothing didn't worry you too much, Marçel,' smirked Sam. 'Where are you now?'

'On the Bombah Broadwater. She has confirmed her name is Sophie, and she's just gone below to clean up and put on some of my clothes.' Marçel added, 'She's a lovely girl, Sam.'

'Don't get carried away, mate. This is a very serious situation and Sophie could still be in grave danger from these killers. I have almost finished here and I reckon the lads can carry on without me. Keep going to Nerong and I will catch you up in the police launch. So don't panic if you see a fast boat coming up behind you.'

'You will have a job to catch up with me, Sam. Wow, but

Sophie's about to catch up with me; she's wearing my shorts and is looking stunning so take your time, mate.' He laughed, 'But seriously Sam, she has had one hell of a bad time with those bastards.' He added, 'I thought it better for you to tell her about the other girl.'

'You're doing well, Marçel mate, but keep your mind on the job and leave the questioning to me. That's an order. See you at Nerong. I will have a police car to take Sophie to headquarters from there.'

Sam felt a great sense of relief. At least the English girl was safe but he was still upset at the loss of the lovely young Aboriginal girl.

Sophie appeared on deck wearing Marcel's rolled-up dark blue shorts. That girl would look stunning in anything, Marcel thought.

'You look great in my shorts, Sophie. They will never be the same after this,' he laughed.

'That's good. At least you will remember me. Thank you for rescuing me. I've had a pretty bad few days.' Sophie paused for a second and added seriously, 'You're my knight in shining armour.'

'I'm very relieved to have found you safe and still alive,' Marçel said quietly.

'You mean you have found the other girl's body?' she asked earnestly as she looked up at him.

Marçel realised he now had to tell her. Maybe it was better this way. He held her hand and spoke quietly to her.

'I am afraid so, Sophie. She must have been a lovely girl,' he sighed.

'She certainly was lovely and also very brave.' Sophie was unable to control the tears that ran down her face. Marçel passed her his handkerchief and she wiped her eyes.

'I think you were both very brave, Sophie.' He put his arm around her shoulder and, quietly sobbing, she buried her face in his arms. After a few minutes she stopped crying and looked up at Marçel and smiled. 'You said you were looking for me. Are you a policeman?'

'No. Not exactly, I'm just helping the police with their inquiries. I am actually here on holiday. I'm in the army back home. I came to Australia on holiday for a few weeks and was having a very relaxing time up until a few days ago ...' Marcel stopped there, thinking it better to wait until Sam joined them before taking the conversation any further.

'I came out here to follow some very nasty people,' Sophie said. I had hoped to catch them out doing something really bad. But that's another story.'

Sophie then gave Marçel a brief account of her experience in the last few days since she had been ambushed at the camping site on the lake.

'So you actually witnessed the murder of the other girl?' Marçel asked. 'That must have been shocking for you. I think you must have a guardian angel; you are very lucky to be here.'

'That's not half of it. Back in London, I witnessed the murder of two other girls. The police gave up on the job, so I decided to follow them up myself.' Sophie paused. 'It's very strange that I keep witnessing girls being murdered. That's three now. They say things happen in threes. Do you think I might be carrying some sort of jinx?'

'I would say not,' Marcel laughed. 'You look much too sensible for that kind of superstition,' he added. And much too lovely, he thought.

'I'm a solicitor you see,' Sophie explained, 'though I have only been practising a short time. But I'm determined to bring this evil fellow solicitor to justice. I followed him here all the way from London.'

'You sound like a very brave girl. And a very determined one.' This was his kind of woman, Marcel decided.

Sophie suddenly froze, spotting something on the horizon behind them. She jumped up, covered her mouth and thrust out her finger.

'Look! Oh my God, Marçel, I think we are the ones being followed now. I wonder if it's …'

Marcel laughed. 'Don't worry Sophie. It's the police boat. They're coming to help us. We are going to meet them nearby in a place called Nerong.'

Sophie slumped back into the seat. 'That's a relief.' She sighed and took a deep breath, looking around her and then turning back to Marçel. 'But it is so lovely here, don't you think? All this water surrounded by forests.'

As they got closer to Nerong, they passed through one of the most beautiful parts of the lake system, with paperbarks and swamp mahoganies leaning over the water, and wetland forests extending right up to the surrounding hills.

Marcel pulled the cruiser up alongside the small jetty at Nerong. Sophie leaped ashore with the ropes and made sure the boat was tied to a close-by bollard.

Within minutes, the police boat had joined them, and Sam jumped across onto the deck of Marçel's cruiser. The police launch then pulled away, leaving them alone.

Sam shook Sophie's hand. 'I'm so pleased you are safe. We have been very worried about you, especially after finding the other girl. Marçel said that you know about that.'

'I guess I have been very lucky but I should never have got myself into this situation in the first place.' Sophie felt embarrassed and slightly angry with herself. 'So what happens now, detective?'

'I'll take you to the Raymond Terrace Police Station for a short interview. Then we'll put you up in a motel close by, with someone posted outside to protect you, of course. Then I'll come and collect you tomorrow morning, and there'll be more interviews at the police station for the rest of the day.' Sam gave her a warm smile. 'After that you can have your car back, but until we have rounded up these killers you are going to need some protection, Sophie.' He put out his hand. 'You can call me Sam.'

'How do you intend to protect me, Sam?' Sophie smiled sweetly.

'Maybe I could do that?' Marçel cut in, realising he was blushing a little. His embarrassment was noted with amusement by Sophie.

'That's not a bad idea, Marçel; that way she can sleep on your cruiser rather than having to stay at the motel. It's more … intimate, no?'

Sophie broke out in a big smile and nodded eagerly.

The detective continued in a severe tone, 'But you know, Sam, you would have to stay with her all the time and keep a watch-out for these criminals. I really think she might be in danger until we catch these people.'

'I would like that.' Sophie was still smiling enthusiastically. 'I mean, I would prefer to stay here than at a motel. Are you sure there is room for me on board, Marçel?'

'No problem,' Marçel replied. 'There are two cabins and two bathrooms. And you will most certainly be safe with me.'

Sophie felt excited at the idea. 'I will give you a call as soon as I'm done at the police station. I'll have my car, so I'll just drive up here.'

'On reflection,' Sam cut in, 'these men know your car. I think it would be better for us to keep it at the station for now. I will bring you up to Bulahdelah myself when we are finished at Raymond Terrace. You're going to need a good long rest after your experience with these maniacs.'

'Don't worry about me, Sam,' Sophie laughed. 'I feel better already. Who's for coffee?'

'Count me in,' said Sam, stepping off the boat with his mobile phone. 'Just excuse me a minute whilst I call my superior and bring him up to date.' He walked over to a park bench and talked for several minutes while Sophie and Marçel prepared a jug of extra-strong coffee.

'When all this is over, you should think about resting right here on the lakes,' Sam suggested to Sophie. 'After talking to my chief, it seems we have quite a serious situation to deal with now. Also I expect the press will be waiting to get hold of your story and will be looking for you. We certainly don't want that to happen until we know exactly who we are looking for. We still don't know what these people are doing here and I'm told that the situation could have some serious international implications.' Sam paused whilst he drank his coffee.

'To be on the safe side, we'll keep you out of sight whilst you are with us. Then I'll bring you here to the cruiser first thing the day after tomorrow and hopefully by then you should be safe from both the crooks and the press.'

'That's fine by me,' said Marçel. 'I look forward to seeing you both the day after tomorrow. I hope you will make sure Sophie is safe and properly looked after at your station.'

'No worries, mate. She'll be safe with us.'

Marcel noticed just how tired Sophie was looking.

'Right Sophie, we had better go now. It is about a

forty-five minute drive to Raymond Terrace. One of our girls will look after you when we get there; she can even nip to the shops and get some clothes for you.'

'Actually, I'm quite happy in Marçel's shorts,' Sophie laughed.

CHAPTER 9

The following morning, Marçel woke up to the raucous sound of several kookaburras initiating some secret joke before being quickly joined by a group of noisy minor birds, friarbirds, purple swamphens, galahs and cockatoos.

Having consumed a bottle of Shiraz the previous evening and woken up with a throbbing head, Marçel was hardly in a state to appreciate the dawn chorus.

But then he remembered Sophie and the image of her brought a smile to his face. Marçel wondered how she was getting on with the police interrogation; it would probably take up most of the day. He felt excited at the thought of her coming back and staying with him on the cruiser. He would have to behave himself and be the perfect gentleman, which would not be an easy task, given how attracted he was to her.

Marçel started the engines, cast off from the Nerong jetty and headed out of the harbour and onto the lake. Over on his right he noticed a smaller backwater and decided to look for a quiet spot where he could stop for breakfast.

Following the twists and turns of this quiet backwater slowly for several miles, Marçel found it interesting that there were no signs of any human habitation in these beautiful surroundings. 'I hope it will always be like this,' he yelled and then listened to the echo of his voice bounce around the strange, isolated place.

The banks on both sides of the little backwater were lined with tall reeds, and behind the reeds paperbarks and also tea-trees, their leaves over many years having stained the waters a light brown, leaned precariously over the water's edge.

Swamp mahogany, she-oaks, gum trees and the occasional palm, mixed with the thick undergrowth, stretched well back from the lake to be gradually replaced by the tall gum trees that covered the hillsides as far as the eye could see.

Marçel eventually reached a point where he found the lake was covered with waterlilies. Rather than risk running aground in shallow water he dropped the anchor, slipped down into the galley, cooked himself a fry-up and with a jug of steaming hot coffee, took his breakfast up to the top deck.

Later, after a swim in the lake, diving off the stern of cruiser and feeling completely refreshed, Marçel decided not to return to Nerong, but to do a complete circle of all the lakes until he found that missing houseboat.

It was at that moment, standing on the upper deck, that he heard a blood-curdling scream coming from somewhere beyond the water lilies. Startled he looked around scanning both sides of the far end of the lake, looking for signs of life.

All he could see were the tall reeds and the paperbark trees; a sea eagle, startled by the sound, flew past followed by several black swans and pelicans, all coming from beyond the water-lily covered area.

Marçel waited a few minutes and then decided that it must have been a bird or perhaps, a trapped and dying animal somewhere in the thick undergrowth. He started the engines, pulled up the anchor and set off back to the main lake.

It was a bright warm sunny day, but it still took Marçel

almost eight hours to circumvent all the interconnecting lakes searching for the missing houseboat.

The endless natural beauty of these lakes fascinated him. In the past, they had been quite busy, with a few small farms and sawmills scattered around, as well as a number of fishing boats and even several tourists who came to visit.

Since then, the whole area had been declared a State Forest; the timber industry had gone, most of the farms and houses had disappeared and tourism, with many excellent camping sites, yachts, small boats and a handful of hotels, had taken their place.

There were areas of shallow water where Marcel was not able to get close to the shore, but he realised that if he could not get there, neither could the houseboat.

Except for the most northern lakes, where there was small gathering of houses and of course Nerong Harbour, the only signs of life were at the few camping spots that were dotted around the lakes and the hotel at Bombah Point where the Bombah Broadwater joined the Myall Lakes.

The few houses he spotted through the trees appeared to be deserted. He realised that at any time the missing houseboat could have crossed the lake behind him and he could have easily missed it. It was late afternoon so he decided not to go back to Nerong, but instead to return to Bulahdelah to see if that houseboat had returned there.

The houseboat hire manager Shaun was standing on the jetty when Marçel came alongside. 'Run short of fuel already, Marçel mate?' he inquired.

'I've been down the river to Tea Gardens and did a complete circle of all the lakes Shaun, so I thought I might as well top up whilst I'm here.' Marçel noticed that there were now three houseboats moored to the jetty. The fourth one, which had been sold, had not returned. It must be still somewhere on the lakes.

'I didn't see a single houseboat on the lakes today.' He took the fuel line from Shaun and connected it to the fuel tank.

'It's been a bit quiet this week. The only hired one that was still out came in last night, but you should have seen the houseboat that we sold the other day; there are several small creeks tucked away well out of sight where they could be.'

'It's not at Tea Gardens. I was told that it's been far too rough the last few days for it to have gone out from the river into Port Stephens,' he added.

For a moment Shaun wondered why all that interest in that particular houseboat but then dismissed the thought. Marçel was just making conversation, he decided.

Marçel passed back the fuel line and paid for the fuel. 'I would like to hire one your kayaks whilst I'm here, Shaun.'

'Just help yourself, Marçel. We won't charge you for that; just make sure you bring it back in one piece. Do you need any fishing gear?'

'No thanks Shaun, I just like to have my fish served on a plate!'

Marçel loaded the kayak on the side deck of the cruiser; there were some very big evil fish he wanted to catch at present he mused. He wandered up to the Plough Inn for a well-earned schooner or two of ale.

★

That night lying in his bunk unable to sleep, Marçel kept wondering what had happened to that houseboat. Why had he not seen it, and was there really a connection to the dead woman?

Something was worrying him. His thoughts wandered

back to that terrified scream he had heard early that morning, when he was about to leave that strangely silent lake near Nerong.

He tried to visualise the scene he had seen the previous morning. He thought about that large area of water lilies. Then he remembered that there was a gap of about three metres running down through the centre of the lilies. There was no reason for this gap, unless perhaps it had been made by a boat passing through. He decided to go and have another look in the morning. With pleasant thoughts of Sophie in his tired mind, he drifted-off into a deep and happy sleep.

The next morning the sky was overcast; Marçel finished his breakfast and set off down the river. This north section of the Myall River from Bulahdelah – about eleven miles – flows into the Bombah Broadwater. Once there, Marçel had to circle a large area of shallow water before reaching the entrance to the small lakes and Nerong. Another three and a half miles of beautiful small uninhabited lakes would take him to Nerong Harbour.

Well before reaching Nerong Harbour, Marçel turned off to the left and headed for the backwater.

He dropped the anchor just a little way short of the water lilies and in just his shorts, a singlet and an Aussie peaked cap, launched the kayak and slowly paddled up the clear channel that ran between the waterlilies.

He paddled down the narrow channel for about a mile scanning the banks of this small waterway.

The whole of the bank was screened by two or three yards of reeds and behind were the paperbarks and she-oaks. He reached the end of the narrow channel and was faced with an area of extra tall reeds. He was about to give up when he realised, looking carefully at the reeds, that they were in fact triglochin procera or 'water ribbons', a type of reed that actually floats in the water. Marçel had encountered these once before when training in Bosnia. At that time they had used the reeds to conceal guns on the lakeside during a training exercise.

Marçel paddled over to the water ribbons and slowly edged the kayak between the tall reeds. He discovered they extended up another even narrower channel for another ten yards before it turned sharply to the left and continued for another hundred yards when they disappeared behind a steep hillside.

He paddled cautiously to the bend, keeping close to the tall reeds on either side of the narrow channel. As he rounded the bend, he saw the houseboat moored in the centre of a large pool, which was roughly fifty yards in diameter.

The pool was surrounded by tall reeds which must have stretched for several yards between the water and the bank. On the bank surrounding the pond, paperbarks hung out over the reeds and behind them were tall gum trees that concealed the steep hillsides.

Marçel reversed the kayak into the reeds and sat quietly watching the houseboat. It appeared to be deserted. He was just about to paddle across to the vessel when the roar of an outboard motor shattered the silence. A large inflatable launch came bursting through the reeds from the other side of the pool; it tore across the water and headed straight for him. It struck the kayak just in front of his feet with such force that he was hurled into the water. An arm came down from the boat; he put up his hand to grab it, but the man with the arm was holding a revolver. The last thing that Marçel remembered was a sudden sharp pain – then blackness.

★

It was late afternoon when Marçel finally came to. He had a splitting headache and an excruciating pain in his back. He was lying on his side on the stern deck of the houseboat. His shoes had been removed and his wrists and ankles were tied closely together behind his back; hence the excruciating pain.

He also realised he was inside a heavy net bag attached to a rope that ran up to the heavy pole above him and which extended out from the side of houseboat.

'So Marçel old boy, you just had to come and visit us. It's such a pity for a fine young army officer like you, to be cut off in the prime of life.' Paul got up from his chair, walked over to Marçel and kicked him in the back.

Marçel gave a little grunt, but by now his back was starting to become numb and he hardly noticed that extra pain.

'You were expecting me.' It was a statement and not a question. 'How did you know I was here?'

'Simple, you asshole.' Kenny stepped over and emptied a bucket of water over Marçel. 'We set up a camera to focus on the waterlily entrance to this place. Our partner got a tip-off about you, when he called into the pub in Tea Gardens.' Charles had been following the activities of the local police and had called into the pub to listen to the local gossip. He decided to use his mobile phone to warn Paul and Kenny that an Englishman was looking for them.

Paul cut in. 'You must realise, Marçel; we can't let you go now. You are a smart guy and you were just lucky to spot the entrance to this lagoon, but no one else will. If they did, we would be long gone. In fact, old boy, this is just our parking spot for the houseboat. Our actual base is at another part of the lake and cannot possibly be detected by boat or even a searching aircraft.'

Paul turned to Kenny. 'Shall we give him a little trial dip?'

'Why not? Time we gave ourselves a little entertainment.'

Paul picked up the rope that ran out over the pulley and down to the net. 'I'll need a hand with this, Kenny.'

As they tightened the rope, Marçel was dragged across the deck, and lifted over the coaming. The net swung out away from the houseboat, leaving him just a few inches above the dark water.

The two men fastened the rope to a cleat on the deck and went back inside the houseboat. Paul tossed a can of beer to Kenny as they relaxed in their deck chairs knocking back their beers whilst Marçel hung out over the lagoon.

Marçel stared up at the rope above him and noticed that it was tied to the drawstring of the net, but there was not another knot on the drawstring. He realised that if he was free in the net when it was underwater, his weight would no longer be on the rope. He might be able to pull back the drawstring and slip out of the net.

He could feel that the knots tying his hands to his ankles were not very tight, but he knew that when they were wet they would tighten and he would be unable to free himself. By the time the two men had finished their drinks, Marçel had managed to slightly loosen the knot around his wrists.

'We decided to have a short rehearsal, Marçel. It will give you the chance to see what drowning really feels like.' Kenny laughed.

Marçel realised that they were just getting a sadistic pleasure out of torturing him before killing him. As they started to lower him into the water, he took a deep breath and when under the water he worked furiously, on trying to free his wrists.

As the seconds passed Marçel felt his lungs were about to burst and he found he was no longer able to struggle to free himself. When on the verge of passing out and when his lungs were about to fill with water, they pulled him up enough to allow his head to appear above the water; he was able to breathe again.

'How was that, Marçel? Did you enjoy?' Paul laughed. 'We will give you time now to reflect on your short misspent life, whilst Kenny and I return your cruiser to the Nerong Harbour.'

It was starting to get dark; Marçel watched as the inflatable launch glided quietly out of the lagoon, towing his kayak. He was by now starting to feel very cold, so he immediately started work on loosening the rope around his wrists.

It was a long and painful process as the knots had now shrunk. He had just freed his wrists when he heard the launch coming back.

Marçel quickly loosened the ropes fastening his ankles, re-tied his wrists to give the appearance of being still trussed up. He was now quite warm after the exertion of freeing himself; he closed his eyes and waited.

Paul brought their launch alongside Marçel's cruiser and climbed on board, attached Marçel's kayak to the side of the cruiser, pulled up the anchor and started the engines.

'Wait around here for thirty minutes at the most, and then bring the launch to that landing spot just around the corner from the harbour. If I'm not there, come quietly through the woods to see what has happened to me,' Paul explained to Kenny.

Paul brought the cruiser with the engines just ticking over, to the Nerong Harbour entrance. He cut the engines and allowed the cruiser to drift to the jetty. It was very unusual for anyone to be at the jetty after dark in this quiet village. He tied up to the jetty, leaving the kayak in the water tied to the cruiser and took the path through the bush back to where Kenny was waiting.

'That was a piece of cake, Kenny. There was not a soul about. When the locals see the cruiser and the kayak there in the morning, they will assume that the owner was picked up by someone with a car and will probably come back later in the day. However, I'm sure the police will put two and two together and guess that we are not too far away from here.'

Kenny started the outboard. 'Guess it's time for plan-B, Paul. We had better get rid of this Marçel guy, and then move on to the main camp. Pity to leave all the grog on the houseboat, but it sure was a good idea drilling and bunging those holes in the floats in case we had a situation like this.'

When they returned to the houseboat, Paul fastened the inflatable and they dived into the main cabin. Kenny opened a fresh bottle of Bourbon and poured two generous glasses. He knocked back his full glass and refilled it immediately.

Paul peered over the side of the boat to check up on Marçel; he was pleased to see Marçel appeared to be asleep. He re-joined Kenny in the cabin, made himself comfortable on one of the armchairs and emptied his glass, which Kenny quickly topped up again.

An hour later with an empty bottle in front of them they got up and staggered to the side of the houseboat. 'Looks like the bugger's dead already. He must have died after we pulled him out of the water, Kenny,' Paul slurred.

Marçel had heard them coming so he lay back in the net, his eyes closed, almost, but with just his nose above water.

'Better make quite sure, Paul,' Kenny chuckled. He untied the rope and allowed the net to sink out of sight in the dark murky water. 'Cum-arne now, let's 'ave another bottle before we get rid of the body, and then move out of here, Paulie boy.'

'You stupid ape, we have to move out before it gets light.'

Kenny struck him on the side of the head; the force of the blow sent Paul over the rail and into the water. He swam around to the stern where Kenny was waiting to help him out. 'You asked for that one, Paulie. No one calls me that.' He laughed. 'Cum 'an' 'ave that drink – stupid!'

★

By the time, the weighted net touched the bottom of the lagoon, Marcel had freed himself from the ropes and was struggling to loosen the rope that kept the net closed.

Suddenly there was a splash above him; he saw two kicking legs before they quickly disappeared. His lungs were near to bursting but he managed to open the net and wriggle out. Fortunately he rose to the surface at the same time that Kenny was helping Paul out of the water at the stern end of the houseboat and Marçel was able to swim out of sight of the two men.

Marçel could hear their voices and laughter coming from the houseboat. They didn't notice him quietly swimming over to the thick reeds. He pulled himself through the reeds and climbed up onto the bank. He lay there for a minute recovering his breath before moving silently away into the bush.

He had only gone a short distance when he heard a shout. 'The bastard got away!'

139

They scanned the pond and the surrounding area with their searchlight but Marçel was lying under a bush as the powerful flashlight passed him by. Shortly after, he heard the outboard motor start; he guessed they would search the pond area and then head up through the reeds to the water lilies and scan both banks on the way to the lake.

Marçel decided to take the least obvious way back to Nerong. The obvious way was to head up towards the lilies and then run along the west bank until eventually he arrived at the Nerong Harbour.

The less obvious way was to first move away from the water, and then head north along the east side of this backwater. After about one mile, just keeping the water in sight, he should arrive at the water's edge which was almost opposite the Nerong Harbour. He would then be faced with about an eight-hundred-yard swim across to the harbour.

It should be light by then so there would be little danger of meeting up with Paul and Kenny, as they would not dare to risk being seen in daylight and in full view of Nerong Harbour.

Moving quickly through the thick bush, Marçel soon realised that without shoes he was going to cut his feet to pieces on the rough surface, but under the circumstances that was a small price to pay. He was more than five hundred metres from the water when he decided to turn left and head parallel to the lake. He used all his army tracking skills to get himself to that point opposite Nerong.

The ground was wet underfoot as it was only a few inches above the level of the lake; there were a few stones and the rough surface of the land, and there was a good covering of dead leaves and rotten branches. This helped to save

Marçel's feet and also helped to deaden the sound of his movement through the bushes.

Twice he heard the launch running up the lake and twice he heard it coming back. He guessed they must be moving out.

After about a mile, he stopped to listen. Not a sound came from the water but close by he heard a slight rustle coming from the bushes behind him.

He froze. In the very faint light, he saw two red eyes and just a little way below were two smaller eyes. Then suddenly two much taller red eyes joined them.

Marçel realised he was looking at a family of kangaroos, mum with her Joey in her pouch and followed by dad the big male. Then with a crash and several thumps on the ground they were gone.

Marçel had to laugh and was quickly joined by a pair of kookaburras who decided to share the joke. It was a hard walk, with so many small tree trunks growing close together and with the thick, sometimes prickly undergrowth, which resulted in forcing him to make many small detours. All the time he kept the water in sight, as it would be so easy for an unskilled person to get lost in this situation.

By the time he reached the edge of the lake, opposite the Nerong Harbour, it was almost daylight. He heard the sound of the inflatable approaching again. Marçel ducked behind a bush and watched as it came speeding around the corner.

It was heavily laden; he guessed they must be moving the last of their equipment to another site on the lake. He felt it was safe now to swim to Nerong; the launch was heading down the lake and would soon disappear out of sight.

★

Paul and Kenny had already made two trips to their new hideout, transferring all the necessary tools including a collapsible hand cart, and of course all the food, bedding and grog that remained on the now sunken houseboat.

'I guess we will never find that bugger now. I just hope he doesn't find us,' Paul yelled as they turned into the lakes, leaving Nerong Harbour behind.

'We really are chancing it, Paul,' cried Kenny. 'It's broad daylight now and there could be local boats around watching where we go.'

'Don't worry Kenny, if I see any other boats I will keep going past the place.'

This time they were lucky. No other boats were in sight and they were able to conceal the launch and carry everything up to the cave without being seen.

They both realised that letting Marçel escape had now blown their cover. But they knew they still had a good chance of getting safely away with the gold. But from now on they must remain out of sight anywhere near the cave until they were ready to leave.

All the gold would soon be packed, ready to transfer to the launch, except for the nuggets that they had carefully dropped in the water at their well-marked spot in the lake.

They were now just waiting to hear from Charles to tell them that he was ready to meet them with the trailer at the camping site. He would give them their final instructions and their departure time from the beach to Broughton Island.

★

Marçel's skin was badly scratched; his feet were sore, but surprisingly not cut. He had dozens of mosquito bites all over his arms, legs and neck.

He scanned the lake; there was not a soul in sight so

he discarded his shirt and trousers, and lowered himself into the water. Something long and slimy brushed past his legs; he guessed it must be one of the thousands of eels that inhabited the lakes.

The water was cold so he kept swimming at a fast rate until he felt himself warming up, alternating with forty strokes freestyle and forty breaststrokes.

By the time he arrived at the slipway, Marçel felt very tired but exhilarated after his long swim. With no one in sight, he climbed up onto the cruiser, which Paul had left moored to the jetty the previous night.

He was surprised to find Sam sitting in the saloon with an anxious look on his face.

'Where the bloody hell have you been? It was just by chance we called in here on our way to meeting you at Bulahdelah and we found your abandoned cruiser here.'

Sophie appeared from the spare cabin.

'Oh my God, where on earth have you been? You are scratched all over and have a nasty wound on your shoulder. We have been so worried about you, and we were just about to start searching the lakes for you.'

'Ah. Yes. Well. I just ran into a hornet's nest yesterday but I managed to get away during the night. Guess I need a shower, guys. Then maybe some breakfast.' He paused. 'Then I will tell you all about my contact with the enemy!' Sophie blocked his way flinging her arms around him unable to express her relief at his safe return.

'Yes, you do look a bit on the rough side,' she laughed, 'but thank God you're back – because I want to stay on your boat, matey.'

Shaved, showered and dressed in clean shorts and T-shirt, and eager to get to the tantalising smell of fresh coffee, ham and eggs, Marçel quickly joined Sophie and Sam in the saloon.

Sophie had been busy in the galley and the three of them tucked into a full English breakfast.

Marcel told them, brushing aside the less pleasant details, about his encounter with Paul and Kenny and their houseboat. 'I don't know what has happened to the third man. I get the feeling that something very sinister is going on here and these two vile men are just pawns in a much larger game.'

'It's pretty obvious to me that it was more than just good luck that you were able to get out of that situation alive,' said Sam thoughtfully. 'Now you know the sort of animals we are dealing with.'

Sophie realised that she was rapidly falling in love with this man; he had been on her mind most of the night and she was excited at meeting him again this morning.

'Take your top off, Marçel; I'm going to put a dressing on that shoulder wound. It's not looking too good. Those scratches also need a bit of a rub with antiseptic cream, I reckon.' As she was saying that, Sophie realised just how much she wanted to touch that strong muscular body; she looked down to hide a blush.

'It's not that bad. I usually heal quickly,' Marçel blurted, though he also wanted to feel her hands touching him. He knew he had fallen for her when she had first come aboard the cruiser two days ago. As Sophie's gentle hands stroked his shoulder, Marçel felt himself close to purring like a cat!

Sam's angry reaction to his description of events surprised him a little.

'I guessed that's what you were going to do yesterday; that's why I left you to search the lakes for the houseboat.

Looking for it was fine, but when you went off on your own to investigate that scream you should have called us first. We might have nailed the bastards. You were very lucky this time, Marçel, but make absolutely bloody sure you contact me first the next time you pull a trick like that.'

Marçel thought about it before replying. He knew Sam was right.

'I guess I underestimated these chaps. Don't worry Sam, this will not happen again; I now have a very personal interest in these thugs and we must definitely work together in finding these killers.'

'I'm sending one of our police patrol boats to take a look at that backwater, Marçel. The houseboat must still be there, but it'll be at least another couple of hours before my chaps can get there. So in the meantime I will organise a chopper to go and take some pictures of the place.'

Marçel and Sophie exchanged a loving glance. Sam stood up. 'Ah well, children, I can see I'm not wanted here.' He laughed.

'I'm off to the station. I think it is time we searched the lakes with the chopper. The lads can search the houseboat and the surrounding area, but I'm sure the crooks are long gone. But where are the buggers? We have got to find them.' Sam gave a long sigh of frustration.

'Still,' he continued after a few seconds, 'with the aid of the chopper searching the lakes, we might just get a clue as to where these devils are.'

'I'll take the cruiser back to Bulahdelah,' Marçel offered. 'It will be safer there. But then I'm going to need some sleep. And now, gosh, I have a lovely nurse to look after me.' Marçel grinned and lightly touched Sophie's shoulder.

Sam stepped down onto the wharf.

145

'I will call you tomorrow morning, Marçel. Go back now and have a good rest; and try to behave yourself this time. And that goes for you too, Sophie.' Sophie gave the inspector a cheeky grin.

Sam jumped into his car and disappeared up the hill.

'You heard what he said, Marçel. We have to behave ourselves; what a waste!' Sophie murmured. 'I think Sam is a really nice policeman,' she added.

Marçel was not quite sure how to take that remark!

'Sophie, can you let go the mooring ropes?' Marçel noted she handled the mooring ropes like an experienced sailor. He started the engines and they backed out from the wharf and motored out of the harbour into the lakes. 'We should get to Bulahdelah in about two hours' time.'

Marcel was surprised that Paul had returned the cruiser undamaged; he realised they must have been very confident that he would never return to collect the cruiser and so they returned the boat intact, in order to delay a search party being sent out to find him. The thought put a chill up his spine.

''Ow ya goin', Mattie?' Sophie asked in a most dubious Aussie accent as she joined him on the upper deck.

'Would you like to take over?' He stood back to let her take the steering wheel.

'Just keep going down the middle of these small lakes. I see you are quite at home driving this ship!'

'When I was at university, I had a boyfriend whose family kept a small cruiser at Weymouth in Dorset,' Sophie explained. 'His name was John and when one day he took me down to meet his parents, they kind of adopted me and I became part of the family They spent a lot of time, especially in the summer holidays, cruising along the coast and across to the Channel

Islands and St. Malo in Brittany. I soon became one of their sailing crew.' Sophie sighed.

'We did a few trips to Jersey, Guernsey, Alderney and Sark and other small ports around the Brittany Coast. Happy days.'

Sophie continued. 'John and I were always good friends but there was really no spark between us. As they say in Australia, we were just good mates.' She looked thoughtful for a moment searching her mind for something to say regarding that friendship.

'John suddenly decided to leave Oxford and join the army. So we were out of touch for some time. Then, one day, when I was on board his parents' yacht in Weymouth, John suddenly appeared with a girlfriend and calmly announced that he had received a commission in the army and was also engaged to marry this lovely girl, Jenny.'

Marçel was struck by a sudden thought. 'Were they married at a church in Dorchester?'

Sophie was silent for a moment. 'But yes. Of course that's it!' she yelled in delight.

'That's it. Good lord!' Marçel was laughing. 'I knew we had seen each other a long time ago.'

'I was one of the bridesmaids and you were one of the guards that were lined up when they came out of the church. I remember thinking that you were dishy then, but never got around to talking to you at the reception. Then you disappeared,' she laughed.

Marçel continued, 'I remember at the time wondering how I could get to talk to you. But I had to leave the reception early as I was going overseas the next day and had to get back to London early that evening.' They were both silent for a few minutes absorbing the facts. Then suddenly they both spoke at the same time. 'That's too much of a coinci …' Marçel started.

'Coincidence!' Sophie finished.

They burst out laughing. 'I just don't believe this is happening. Can it really be the same Sophie?'

Marçel instinctively put his arm around Sophie's shoulder. She let go of the steering wheel and put her arms around him. Marcel bent down and they kissed tenderly to start with, but then the kisses soon became passionate; they were both carried away by this precious moment.

'Oh my God! We are heading for the shore.' Marcel leaped to the controls to cut the motors; then too late he put them into reverse gear. The motors roared and there was a distinct thud as the cruiser's bow cut a deep wedge into the soft mud bank. Marcel cut the two motors; the cruiser was well and truly stuck in the mud.

The sudden silence was broken by first a quiet giggle from Sophie and then roars of laughter from two suddenly love-struck twenty-five year olds.

Marcel's attempts to reverse the cruiser out from the bank failed. They moved every movable object out on to the stern deck of the cruiser hoping to lift the bow out of the mud.

'Okay Sophie. Can you handle the motor controls? If so, I'm getting onto the bank and I will use all my strength to push the boat out of this mud.'

'No problem, Marçel. You jump ashore and when you are ready I will go full speed astern.' Sophie was still finding herself giggling over the situation, and at the same time she also had a feeling of great happiness.

'Right Sophie, I'm ready to push so give it the gun.'

The motors roared and Marcel heaved until he became red in the face with the effort.

All of sudden it shifted a few inches, and then shot back as the bow of the cruiser cleared the mud bank. It happened so fast that Marcel went with the cruiser and promptly fell into the muddy water.

The roar of the motors died and replaced by the renewed howls of laughter from Sophie.

She backed away a few yards from the bank, switched off the motors and went to the stern deck to help Marcel get back onto the boat. As Sophie put her arm down to help Marçel, he gripped her arm and pulled her into the water. They laughed and played around like a couple of kids until they were completely exhausted. Marçel then climbed back on to the deck and heaved Sophie up after him.

'I suppose you will need another pair of my shorts now, you lovely woman.'

'As a matter of fact, young man, I was able to get my things out of my car, so you can have your shorts back, if you want them.'

'Not bothered, darling.' Marçel realised he had called her darling without thinking. 'A first? Maybe he was pushing things forward too fast?'

'Good. I shall keep them and treasure them as my first gift from you.' She laughed.

It was midday when they arrived at Bulahdelah in the brilliant sunshine. Sophie brought the cruiser gently alongside the jetty in a most professional manner and Marçel leaped ashore with the mooring ropes.

'I need to go up to the shops, Sophie, I have to replace my mobile phone which is at the bottom of the lake and we need some fresh food for dinner tonight.'

'Hang on Marçel; I'm coming with you. And I will get the food supplies. This is my contribution as you are kindly letting me stay on your super-yacht. I will be quite happy to take over the cooking. I hope you have a strong stomach!'

Laden with supplies they called in at the pub and after prawn sandwiches and a couple of beers slowly strolled back to the cruiser.

'I would like you to have the State Cabin, Sophie, as it has its own bathroom and also,' Marçel paused and grinned, 'a double bed.'

'Gosh. Thanks.' Sophie ignored the double bed bit. 'And where is the skipper sleeping?' she asked archly.

'Well,' he paused, 'why, the guest cabin darling! Where you slept last night.' It was clear they both had other ideas on their minds.

'Right Marcel. You must be dead beat. Go and get some sleep and I will bring you a cup of tea at 5pm.

At 4 o'clock Sophie peeped into Marcel's cabin to see if he was sleeping. He was.

Unable to resist the temptation she quietly undressed and slipped in beside him. By then, Marcel was very wide awake!

Two hours later, there was a heavy crash on the deck of the cruiser. Sophie leaped up, grabbed a blanket, wrapped it around her and dashed into the State Cabin.

Sam dropped down into the saloon. 'Anyone aboard this vessel?' he shouted.

Marcel appeared from his cabin wearing shorts and his T-shirt.

'Well …' Before Sam could say anything, Sophie appeared from the State Room, wearing a light dress and looking quite innocent.

'I thought the lady should have the cabin with a bathroom,' Marçel murmured. He was unable to disguise that happy look on his face, like the cat that had got the cream.

Sam smiled benevolently at them. 'You both look very happy today; I have some good and bad news for you.'

'There is a bottle of Champers in the fridge, Sam; okay by you?' Marcel brought out the bottle and glasses.

'It's a lovely evening, boys; let's take our drinks to the upper deck.' Sophie realised she felt really happy and safe with these two men.

CHAPTER 10

'So what's the latest, Sam?' Marçel came up the ladder with a second bottle. 'How about that houseboat? Has the chopper found it yet?'

'Yes. It's in the centre of the lagoon; we spotted the roof jutting out of the water in the centre of that pond where you found it. They must have scuttled it. We'll send divers down tomorrow to see if they can patch the floats, pump air into them and re-float the houseboat.'

'So now we are right back where we started,' mused Marçel. 'Surely Sam, there must be some other traces of them somewhere around these lakes.'

'The chopper spotted a few tracks in the mud, so we dropped one of our men to follow the footprint tracks around that part of the lagoon. Some of them, the barefoot ones, must have been yours after you escaped as they ended at the side of the lake where you started your swim to Nerong. The others only went a short distance from the water's edge, except for another set of bare feet and a booted pair which ran along the water's edge on the other side of the lake, then stopped. The booted foot marks returned along the lakeside bank, close to where we found the houseboat.'

Sam was silent for a moment. 'Now this is the bad news – this was where we found him, or rather his dead body.'

'Oh my God; who was it?' Sophie whispered.

Sam continued slowly. 'The victim was a very old man who appeared to be in extremely poor condition. He was filthy dirty and dressed in animal skins. He had long grey hair and a straggly beard that had grown down to his waist. The poor man looked starved; one of his legs was badly swollen and might have even been poisoned, as it was going black. When we examined him we discovered that he didn't have a tongue. It must have been cut out a long time ago.'

'How was he killed?' Marcel asked.

'We think he was stabbed in the back whilst trying to run away.'

'Bastards. When will they stop this killing?' Sophie was furious. 'We really must find them before they kill any more people. How could they slaughter an old man like that.'

'We have no idea who this man is or where he came from. It's very strange that no one has ever reported seeing him before.' Sam seemed extremely upset over this murder.

Marçel got up and stretched. 'So now we are back where we started, Sam. Sophie is quite right. We must nail the bastards before they kill any more people.'

'Not quite. I told you we sent a chopper to see where the houseboat was. While they were there, I told them to examine the shoreline farther down in the Bombah Broadwater.' Sam paused.

'There was nothing to see on the shoreline, but whilst doing a circuit around a small hill about a mile back from the water's edge; they spotted some wheel tracks through the trees that started near the water and ended on the side of the hill. They looked like the wheels of a hand cart and there were quite a lot of them. The cart must have made several journeys up and down the hillside.'

'So what are we waiting for? Let's go and have a look'.

'This could be something or it could just as well be a

dead lead, Marçel. This is an isolated area, I should call for back-up and move in with the 'troops'. But this was just an odd sighting, and it's likely it was nothing at all. A major operation there could send these thugs to ground. So my friend,' Sam stood up, smiled, and then stretched his arms above his head, 'it looks like it's up to you and me.'

'You want us to quietly suss out these wheel marks in the middle of the bush?' Marcel laughed. 'Well, let's go! This is right up my street.'

Then, after some thought, 'but Sam we will need some special equipment for this foray.'

Sam brought in the heavy bag that he had left on deck and tipped the contents onto the table. 'I am really sticking my neck out here, Marçel, but I reckon you are far more capable than any of my colleagues to carry out what might turn out to be, a very dangerous task.'

Marçel rummaged through the contents of the bag. 'Well, you certainly have this part right: a large scale map, a small compass, a two-way radio ... mobile phones ...' he paused, 'they might not work there.'

Still rooting through Sam's holdall, Marçel continued the inventory. 'Two mini First Aid kits, chocolate and water bottles and, wow, two loaded revolvers. How did you manage to sneak them away?'

'With great difficulty. I have spoken to your boss in London and he tells me you are an expert at this sort of thing. I was in the army prior to joining the police and did get quite a lot of bush training. If we find nothing, no one will ever know, and if we are successful, the shit will hit the fan for going it alone; but I can live with that.' He laughed.

'Marçel, the radio will be manned at the station night and

day and I have arranged for the chopper and six fully-armed police to stand by in case we need them in a hurry.'

Marçel was silent for a moment as he contemplated his mission. 'You know this might turn out to be very nasty. Are you prepared to accept me as leader and do everything I ask of you?'

Sam smiled, leaned over the table and shook Marçel's hand. 'This is your show, Marçel. Your word is my command. Lead on, Captain Beaumont!'

Marcel studied the map. He circled an area just a short way from where the upper Nerong River ran into the Broadwater. 'Can you show me the exact spot where the wheel marks were seen?'

Sam pointed to a spot on the opposite side of the Broadwater.

'That's it. At the bottom of the hill, about eight hundred metres from the water's edge. The shoreline dips in quite a lot there. The bush is thick on that side, and has a fairly large area of reeds in front of it. There is a faint unused track on the other side of the hill that runs through the bush for about five kilometres and comes out at a cattle farm.'

'Right. That's fine. We'll leave here one hour before dark, drop the anchor in that small creek at the bottom of the river, by which time it should be dark enough for us to kayak the two miles across to the bank fairly close to where we think these people are.'

The two men nodded in agreement. Marçel looked Sam up and down and frowned. 'Sam, do you have anything more mission-appropriate than that smart suit to wear?' He smiled.

'Yes, I have a tracksuit and trainers in my car. I'll go get them. At the same time, I'll collect a second kayak from the boatyard. There's room for two kayaks on the deck.'

'What about me, guys?' Sophie cut in earnestly. 'Am I coming with you?'

'Sorry Sophie; it was ...'

'Don't you dare say 'boys' business' or I'll thump you,' she grinned.

'Look Sophie, we need somebody to stay on the cruiser in case things go wrong and we have to be picked up in a hurry. I am going to park the cruiser in an out-of-sight place at the bottom of this part of the river. Will you do that for us?'

'Of course Marçel; I realise I'm not trained to follow you chaps and I would probably become a liability to you, but I'd still like to feel like I could be useful.'

'Thanks, Sophie. It'll be good to know you are in charge of the cruiser. Sam will tune in the cruiser's radio so that you can hear any messages he might be sending back to the police station. Besides, we might need you to come and pick us up.'

Sophie stood up, Marçel put his arms around her, held her tightly and they kissed passionately until Sam re-appeared with the second kayak and two small backpacks.

One hour later, as the Australian sun started to sink behind the mountains with darkness soon to follow; they cast off the mooring ropes and set off.

There was a twist in the river one mile before it ran out into the Broadwater, at which point they turned off into a small side-lake. As the light was beginning to fade, they dropped anchor and both men quickly launched and then slipped into their kayaks.

'Sophie, your radio is tuned in to ours; please do not call us as we might be in a dangerous situation where silence is essential.' Marçel gave Sophie a quick wave and started to move away from the cruiser, his mind now completely focused on the job ahead. Sophie leaned over the transom and reached down to give Sam's kayak a push. Sam stretched an arm and managed to squeeze Sophie's hand. 'And don't worry, Sophie dear; I'll bring him safely back to you.'

'You had better do that or else I will come after you with all guns firing!'

Sophie watched as they moved away from the cruiser and started paddling to the river mouth.

'Good luck. And give the bastards one from me!' Sophie yelled after them. 'See ya later mates,' she murmured.' Sophie went back into the saloon. She realised they were dealing with some very clever and deadly criminals. The slight crackle coming from the radio made her feel reassured.

Once on the Broadwater, Marçel checked his compass and they headed due south. The only sound to be heard on this still night was the ripple of water as the bows of the kayaks cut through the still water.

As they approached the opposite shore of the Broadwater, Marçel paddled alongside Sam, speaking quietly, 'If this is the right place, then any chance of success depends on surprise. We both know these are very tough experienced guys; they will show no mercy if they capture us.'

'Whatever you say, boss! I'll just follow behind you and stay very quiet,' Sam hissed.

'Just follow and try to keep about five metres behind me, be as silent as you can when we are moving through the bush. Avoid standing on any small branches – just be ready to flatten yourself in the dirt if you hear or spot anyone coming in our direction.'

They glided slowly towards the thick patch of tall reeds, pulling their way through till they reached the low mud bank. Marçel raised his hand and they stopped and waited for several minutes before climbing up onto the bank, quietly dragging the kayaks up on to the bank with them.

Marçel decided he had to find the place where the crooks concealed their inflatable launch; their tracks would lead up to whatever sort of shelter they had organised for themselves on the hillside.

Should they go left or right? They had come in slightly to the left of their estimated landing place, so they turned to the right, keeping close to the side of the lake. A hundred metres on they came to a narrow channel that ran inland; still keeping on the edge of the bank, they followed this channel for about fifty metres and there, at the very end of the channel, they found the inflatable launch hidden by tree branches that overhung the channel.

Briefly, using his torch, Marçel was able to see that the wheel tracks ran down from the hill and right to the moored inflatable.

The wheel marks in the mud were similar to those of a small two-wheel trolley. They moved quietly back into the bush. 'Let's move up parallel to the track,' Marcel whispered.

They must have travelled about seven hundred metres, picking their way through the thick bush, when suddenly the beam from a powerful torch swept past them as it scanned the area; Marçel froze, then signalled Sam; they slowly sank to the ground and lay crouched on the wet mud waiting.

After a few minutes the light was switched off; Marçel and Sam lay still in the darkness for another fifteen minutes, until Marçel decided it was safe to move on.

They had covered about hundred metres when the light came on again, and again they lay low in the rough grass; this time, however, they were more exposed as they were now in a far more open area. The powerful beam slowly scanned the terrain until it arrived at where they lay. Four shots rang out.

Marçel heard a grunt behind him and knew Sam had been hit. He turned to see Sam crawling towards the cover of a bush. Marcel rolled to the side and crawled forward until he was able to reach another thick bush. Then, to add to his problems, Marçel found he was staring straight into the eyes of a large and extremely lethal-looking brown snake.

He slowly withdrew the sharp pointed bush knife, attached to his belt.

It became a test as to which of them could move the fastest. They both struck-out at the same split second. Luckily, Marçel was just a fraction faster and his knife entered the snake's mouth and came out through the top of its head.

A hand gripped his ankle; he thought it was Sam and then for the second time in forty-eight hours, he received a sharp blow to the head – and once again passed out.

CHAPTER 11

Marçel opened his eyes, water was dripping from his hair and face, and he felt his skull had been split in two. Kenny chuckled as he put down the empty bucket.

Marçel realised that he was tied firmly to a plastic folding chair and in the dim light from a hanging lantern, glanced down at his bare feet; they were resting on Sam's back.

He could feel some warmth against his feet; at least Sam was still alive. Sam's left shoulder and chest were covered in congealed blood, but Marçel could see and feel that Sam was still breathing.

Kicking the bucket out of his way, Kenny firmly gripped Marçel's nose and pushed his head back. Marçel felt the cold steel of Kenny's knife against his throat.

At that moment, Paul stepped forward. 'Say Marçel, how would you like a job training my men? I guess we could use a guy like you in our organisation,' he laughed as he grabbed Marçel's hair and pulled back his head, away from Kenny's threatening knife. Marçel could smell his revolting stale breath.

'Guess you almost made it this time, Marçel. It would be such a pity to waste those talents and all your expensive army training.'

'Where are all these men?' Marçel slurred, 'I just don't see any of them around.'

Paul kicked him on the shin.

'Paul was in the army once,' Kenny growled. 'They kicked

him out because Paul was too hard on his men, poor buggers, and in the end he was caught screwing the colonel's wife. You certainly messed up there, Paul; but it was lucky for you they chucked you out, mate. You would never have gained any respect from your men.' Kenny slowly made two deep scratches on Marçel's shoulder before returning his knife to its sheaf.

'I was never in the bloody army, nor would I ever want to be,' he growled. 'All that discipline and bull-shit's not for me.'

'If you had been in the British Army and in my platoon, your feet would never have touched the ground,' Marçel spat, his anger almost getting the better of him. 'I would have trained your body and mind to the very limit and then far beyond; you might even have become a real man. But I'm afraid it's far too late now for an animal like you.'

Kenny laughed, but realised this man was probably right. If he had been drafted into the Marines at an early age, his spirit would have been crushed and he would never have made the big time, which is where he hoped he would soon be, when this job was over and he had a stack of cash to spend.

The thought suddenly flashed before Kenny that he might find it hard to kill Marçel when the time came; however, this guy was the first person to challenge and almost get the better of him; so he decided there was no alternative and he had to die.

'I guess you have almost reached your peak in the army, Marçel,' Paul continued, 'and then after that, I suppose its downhill all the way to your retirement or discharge. I expect you'll probably end up with just a small pension for your old age.'

Paul realised that if it was only Marçel that was

preventing them from getting out of this situation, perhaps with a promise of sum of the gold he might be persuaded to join them and help them get away He looked down at other guy, lying at his feet and decided he would soon be dead anyway.

'My pension is not that small,' Marçel managed a smile, 'and my needs are pretty modest.'

'Yes, but working for me, you could very soon become filthy rich.'

'Or just very filthy,' Marçel retorted.

Paul gave up on the idea.

'Better than being very clean and very dead.' Kenny struck Marçel a heavy blow across the face with the back of his hand, causing his nose to bleed.

Paul picked up his revolver and headed for the door.

'I'm going down to check the launch and to make sure there were no others that were supporting these two men,' Paul told Kenny. 'They could be waiting down by the waterfront. He slipped out of the bunker, closing the steel door behind him.

Marçel felt a slight movement under his foot. Sam was coming to. Marçel gently moved his foot against Sam's back to let him know he was there. He hoped Sam would remain silent and not reveal that he had regained consciousness.

★

Sam was not happy; he was following right behind Marçel and lying on his stomach in the thin layer of the mud that covered this part of the rainforest. He realised just how unfit he had become in these last few years since joining the police force. He'd had no regrets since leaving the army; he had enjoyed every moment in the Police Force and was ambitious to climb the ladder, even though it had made it very difficult for him to have a serious female relationship. Plenty of time for that in the future Sam reckoned.

They were working their way close to the side of the wheel tracks, although it was making it easier for them to move forward without the obstruction of the thick undergrowth, they were now far more exposed.

They were getting nearer to the hill when the tracks were suddenly bathed in the light from a very powerful lamp.

For what seemed like several minutes, they lay frozen on the ground. The light went off and after another fifteen minutes, they again started to slowly move forward.

The brilliant light returned. This time they realised they were completely exposed and could be clearly seen.

From just a few yards ahead of them, several gunshots pierced the still night. Sam stifled a scream as the bullet pierced his left shoulder; for just that split second, it felt as if he had been pinned to the ground by the impact.

Sam was left in darkness as the light was now searching the track for Marçel. Realising they were now in deep trouble and were going to need help, taking advantage of the temporary darkness Sam, with his good arm, managed to slowly withdraw his two-way radio from his jacket. He switched it on and called the duty officer at his headquarters in Raymond Terrace. A weary voice answered. In little more than a whisper, Sam gave his name to the officer on duty, told him to alert the officers on standby and tell them to move in to the target at dawn.

He pushed the radio under some dead leaves.

Sam did not hear the approaching footsteps as by then he was already unconscious.

His eyes slowly opened, and as his head started to clear, he realised he was still lying in mud but in different surroundings. There were feet resting on his back. He moved slightly and felt the feet give a wriggle. He looked up and saw through the dim light that it was Marçel, who remained completely silent. In a second, Paul understood what Marçel was trying to tell him. He closed his eyes and decided to remain silent and still.

'What are you doing here anyway?' Kenny demanded. Marçel was also wondering why he was in this ridiculous situation!

'That's a strange question, Kenny; I'm sure you know why we are here,' he answered guardedly and continued. 'We found a girl's hand and then later we found her body. I presume that was your work. So we came to find you. And here we are in a cave full of guns and explosives. A cave hidden away on a lakeside hill, in the middle of a State Forest ...'

This took Kenny by surprise. He interrupted Marcel: 'I don't think you really know why we are here.' He paused. 'You just happen to have found a hand, followed it up and by sheer good luck found the girl's body. Well, I'm buggered!'

There was a thump on the steel door at the cave entrance. Kenny crossed over, and opened the cave door. Paul slipped in, slamming the door behind him.

He walked over to Sam who grunted when Paul kicked him in the ribs; then he punched Marçel in the guts and pointed at Sam.

'That one is not dead yet.'

Kenny chuckled. 'Almost. He won't last long anyway.'

'I found two kayaks. There is no one else here; I think we are quite safe for now. But Kenny, our cover is blown and it looks like we might have to abort the whole plan.'

'We can't do that, Paul. Karl has spent a fortune

setting this up. Besides, if we fail now, Karl will hunt us to death. Let us get rid of these two and lie low for a few days. Perhaps these bastards are the only ones who know about this place.'

Paul pulled a gun from his pocket and wiped it on his sleeve; then he pointed it at Kenny. He stood by the door staring silently at the three men.

'I really am pissed off with you, Kenny; you have a brain that would pass through the eye of a needle.' He turned to address Marçel. 'This is your one chance. You can join us now to finish this job or you stay here and die in this cave.'

Marçel managed a weak laugh. 'Piss off, Paul. You know you won't get very far. You'll be tracked down, arrested and locked up for the rest of your life.'

Paul turned his attention to Kenny.

'You messed up when you killed that girl, Kenny. Either the police or that maniac Karl will get to us now.' Paul paused for a moment. 'So I've decided to leave you here to look after these two smart policemen. What you do with them is your decision, but if you are ever found alive; remember there is no mercy shown for killing police officers.'

Paul opened the steel door, slipping the gun back in his pocket as he stepped out of the cave. He slammed the steel door behind him and slid the two outside bolts across the door.

Paul pushed his way through the thick undergrowth concealing the cave entrance and headed down the hill to the launch, leaving the three men trapped inside the cave.

He was not a coward; he had in fact carefully accessed the situation. He rightly concluded that once he and Kenny had delivered the gold to Karl, they would both become a danger to his whole enterprise and both he and Kenny would have to be eliminated. That is, if they managed to finish the job before the police arrived on the scene.

Had everything gone to plan, Charles might have survived but now he was sure that once Charles finished the cleaning-up operation, destroying all evidence of their presence in Australia, he would also be killed.

For that reason he had decided to opt-out and if possible, skip the country. In his jacket pocket there was one bar of gold which he had secretly hidden away whilst they were packing the gold nuggets into the bags and nets; he had done it quickly and Kenny hadn't noticed a thing.

He would use this gold to help him to buy into a job on a freighter that sailed to South America. Once there, he would change his identity and retire safely out of reach from Karl's organisation.

He scrambled onto the launch which was concealed in the narrow channel and almost completely blocked by the floating reeds. He started the powerful outboard motor, He started the powerful outboard motor, which happened to drown out the noise of the approaching helicopter.

The launch slipped out from behind the reeds and into the lake. Paul gave the motor full throttle and headed across the water to the camping site at Mango Brush.

As he came up to the camping site ramp, it suddenly dawned on Paul that Charles had taken the truck and trailer away with him when he had returned to Newcastle.

He wandered around the site and found that there were two other campers in the park. One had a large tent with an even larger four-wheel drive truck parked alongside. As he got nearer, he could hear loud snores coming from inside the tent.

Paul walked over to the other tent, which had another four-wheel drive parked a little way outside.

He decided that this was the one to take. He took out his revolver from his pocket, pulled back the safety catch and opened the tent door. To his surprise, there was no one inside.

As there were no fishing rods around, Paul decided that the tent's occupants must have gone fishing. He searched the contents of the tent and found a set car keys under one of the pillows. Sure enough, they opened the door of the Range Rover outside; Paul jumped into the car and drove out of the camping site.

There were only two choices; to turn left would take him to the ferry, which would not be running until well after dawn but it was a little-used road and would have given him his best chance of getting away from any police patrol. To turn right meant driving to Hawks Nest, crossing over the bridge to Tea Gardens and then just following the road until he came to the main highway – a much faster way, but there might be more people around as it would soon be daylight. He turned right, deciding that if he went fast, he could be on the highway before daylight.

All went well and Paul passed over the Hawks Nest Bridge without seeing anyone, and the road through Tea Gardens was also deserted. Paul started to relax; he would soon be on the highway. About halfway along the road from Tea Gardens to the highway, he saw a row of headlights coming towards him.

The police were answering Sam's call for help, and they had also received a mobile phone message form a distraught lakeside camper who had reported that his Range Rover had been stolen.

Too late, Paul realised that both lanes were blocked and he was forced to stop. One police car blocked his way and the other one drew up alongside. Paul reached for his gun and then saw that both the police car windows were open and two guns were now pointing directly at him.

Minutes later Paul found himself handcuffed and sitting in the backseat of the car with a police officer, heading over to the Raymond Terrace Police Station. The rest of the convoy continued down to Tea Gardens where they were to meet up with the police launch and the helicopter.

★

Kenny stood open-mouthed staring at the closed door, and then he let out a piercing scream of rage as his slow brain took in the situation. They were trapped inside the cave, and his partner had deserted him.

'Well Kenny, that's a turn up for the books! Now we really are in the poo.' Marçel stood up and hopped over to the door. He examined it carefully and shook his head. 'You got the keys, Kenny?' He smiled.

'I'll kill ya. Ya bastard, you know there ain't no keys. He's bolted the bloody door.' He bent down and picked up his gun, which had fallen to the floor when Paul had entered the cave and pointed it at Marçel.

'Yes, you can do that, Kenny. That's definitely an option. But if you kill me, you will never get out of this cave alive and if you ever did, you wouldn't last long after killing two police officers. You can untie me now – I'll not be going anywhere for a while and you are going to need my help to get out of here.'

Kenny, his hands shaking badly, produced his lethal pocket knife and cut him free.

Marçel was surprised to see such a look of fear on Kenny's face. Kenny was suddenly wondering whether Australia still had the death penalty. He was an extremely tough criminal who rarely showed signs of fear, but confinement in the cave and fear of the electric chair were taking their toll on him.

'You know there is no way out of this hole unless Paul comes back.' He banged his fists against the steel door. 'I know him. He won't come back.' Kenny was shaking; he sat down with his head between his legs. 'We are going to slowly starve to death. I can't stand being trapped; it's not the same as being in prison. We can never get out of here,' he wailed.

He could be right Marçel thought, if the police team on standby are not able to find the cave entrance. He glanced across at Sam; his eyes were open and his mouth was moving; he was trying to say something. Marçel had been examining the steel door; he moved over to Sam, bent down and put his ear close to Sam's mouth.

'Called – base – coming – dawn,' he whispered, and then Sam passed out again. Marçel carefully examined Sam's wound. He had lost a lot of blood but the bleeding had stopped.

Marçel looked around the cave; he found some dirty stained animal furs in a corner and slipped one under Sam and covered him with another. He looked down at his friend and smiled. 'How's that, tiger?' He decided not to tell Kenny that help was on its way. Let the bastard sweat, he thought.

To pass the time, Marçel wandered over to the stack of cases containing the arms. He wondered if they were still usable after so long.

He found his torch lying on the dirt floor and shone it on the cases. They had all been opened and shining his torch into them he found they all contained live ammunition and hand grenades that were used in the Second World War.

Then he noticed that another five of the ammunition cases had been put to one side, and had also been opened.

169

He put his hand in the case and felt some sort of netting; pulling it out of the case he was surprised at its heavy weight.

He turned around to see Kenny pointing his gun at him, his hand shaking almost uncontrollably. He was glaring at Marçel with a very strange expression on his face.

'Touch that and yer dead.'

Marçel, having no idea of what was in the net bags, backed off from the cases and walked slowly towards Kenny, who brought his other shaking hand up to try and hold the gun steady.

'Whatever is in those boxes, it could be something that we could use to help us escape out of here,' Marçel smiled.

Kenny looked confused; he slowly lowered the gun, and as he did so Marçel stepped forward and snatched it from Kenny's hands, striking him on the side of his head with the metal shaft. Kenny's knees gave way; he sank to the ground and started to weep like a child.

Marçel returned to the five cases. Strange, he thought; it was a net with something very heavy inside. It was definitely not a clip of cartridges. Inside the net there was a heavy canvas bag in which he put his hand and lifted out one of four heavy metal bars. He shone the torch on it.

'My God! So this is what it's all about.'

Marçel examined the gold bar then slipped it back in the bag and replaced it in the case. He turned the torch on to Kenny.

'You bastards came here to steal this gold, which must be worth millions and which must certainly belong to the Australian Government. And you were prepared to kill in order to do this?' He shouted angrily at the grovelling man who was now furiously clawing at the steel door.

'I don't know nuffin' about all this,' Kenny jabbered,

nearly hysterical. 'Jus' ya get me out of this hole … I don't want to die here!'

'You are going to die, Kenny, whether it's in this bunker or outside. And I for one would certainly take great pleasure in killing you. You miserable creature.'

Before Kenny could reply, there was a loud bang on the door, the bolts were pulled back and a group of fully armed policemen stormed into the bunker.

Within seconds, Marçel and Kenny found themselves pinned to the ground, handcuffed and lying on their stomachs.

'That's your officer lying over there,' Marçel managed to point over at Sam. 'He needs to be attended to immediately. Get him to a hospital now!' he thundered.

'Who the hell do you think you are, mate?' The police sergeant in charge looked down at him. He had not known of Marcel as he had been recently transferred from Sydney to Newcastle Police Station.

'I'm here assisting your boss, Detective Sergeant Sam Morrow. He has a gunshot wound. Get your chopper to take him to the nearest hospital before he bleeds to death. And don't let your men touch those cases of gold bullion,' he added.

The sergeant yelled orders to his men. He had assumed the body lying on the ground was dead and realised he should have checked it first. A stretcher appeared from nowhere and within minutes Sam was taken out of the bunker to the chopper that was hovering overhead.

Before Sam's stretcher was hitched to the chopper's cable, he was able to murmur a few words to the sergeant. 'Help my assistant. Arrest that other one and take me to Bulahdelah Hospital. I need to stay close to this case.'

171

The sergeant returned to the bunker, and helped Marçel to his feet, removing his cuffs. 'Sorry about this, sir; we have to be cautious and arrest everyone when we first come in. We tend to then sort everything out afterwards, if you know what I mean. Detective Morrow has just ordered me to help you organise things here and says he hopes to see you later in the morning. He is on his way to Bulahdelah Hospital; I'm sure they can deal with him there.'

'That's okay by me, Sergeant. I'm not in the force; just a Pom helping out! Until Detective Morrow is able to return here, I suggest you take this miserable criminal to Raymond Terrace Jail. You need to put a heavy padlock on the bunker door and keep a man here on duty close by, until Sam – Detective Morrow – is able to resume his duties and return to this bunker.'

Marçel tried not to sound as if he was giving orders to his troops and found that the sergeant was quite happy to go along with his instructions.

'Okay sir; that sounds right. By the way, we have already arrested another one of the gang this morning. He was trying to escape in a stolen car. I told Detective Morrow. I expect it will cheer him up.' He paused. 'But, what about you, sir? Are you all right?' He noticed the cuts on Marçel's arm; will you be returning with us to Raymond Terrace, or do you have your own boat close by?'

'My boat is moored at the bottom end of the upper Myall River.' Marçel felt compelled to add: 'By the way Sergeant, I think the press will want to know all the details of the outcome and also the arrests that have taken place. I'm sure Sam would like you to keep this all secret at this stage. Also, I'm sure the details of the location and contents of the bunker should remain undisclosed until all the criminals have been arrested and the case closed.'

'Of course, sir. That is normal procedure in these cases,' the sergeant replied sharply.

They wandered around the bunker making a rough list of the contents there. 'All these arms ... all that gold ... concealed in this place all those years ago ... I don't understand how this cave could have remained undiscovered for so long, sir.'

'I just wonder what happened to the people that brought all this here. Someone in the services must have given the orders to establish this bunker. The gold must have been delivered at the same time; but where did it come from?' The sergeant scratched his head.

'Sergeant, we are dealing with the lowest kind of criminals. But I'm, sure they must be working for a very large criminal organisation, and it wouldn't surprise me if they have already removed some of these gold bars from the cases and hidden them somewhere outside. I think you should get your men to search the area before you leave this place.'

'I think you are right, sir.'

'That was not an order, Sergeant; just a suggestion.' Marçel laughed. 'And do you mind if I use your police radio to call my boat? My mate will be wondering where I am.'

'Just go for it, sir, and you can tell your mate to put the kettle on.' The sergeant gave Marcel a wink and smiled.

★

'Hi Sophie are you okay? ... Yes I'm fine and we have been very successful and have locked up two of the crooks ... Sam is not too good; he has been taken to a hospital ... Yes, a bullet wound but not too bad ... Yes, I missed you too ... Can you put the kettle on? ... You are? Well, if you think you can manage the cruiser that would be great ... When you come out into the Broadwater, head for the green and red buoys, then turn right and you will see the police boats in the distance. I'll be waiting … Love you too, darling.'

Within minutes the cruiser appeared from the river entrance. Marçel noticed that it expertly circled well clear of the shallow area and then came at full speed across the lake to where the police boats were standing by to take most of the policemen back to Tea Gardens.

Marçel waded out to meet the cruiser and climbed on board as soon as Sophie cut the engines.

'Oh my God, Marcel. You're back! You look filthy dirty, darling, but thank goodness you are in one piece.' Sophie flung her arms around Marçel, transferring his mud to her clothes.

'Sorry I'm so late,' he laughed, turning Sophie's tears into laughter. 'However I'm glad you missed me.' And the long and tender kiss, became a long and passionate kiss.

'Where is Sam? How badly is he hurt? What happened?'

'Sam was wounded. He is now at the Bulahdelah Hospital. We can go and see him later this afternoon, when they have finished sewing him up.' Marcel followed Sophie into the galley.

'You'll be pleased to know that we now have the two killers under lock and key. Unfortunately, Charles, the third man, is still on the loose.'

Sophie passed Marçel a mug of tea. 'He is the one I really want you to catch,' she said, her face suddenly changing to a very serious expression. 'He is a very dangerous man; always in the background organising the killers and making sure they get off when they are caught. He's one wicked bastard.'

'But I do think that in this case, he is just a go-between.'

Sophie agreed. 'He is certainly not the boss. This

has been organised by top criminals and, it seems, with unlimited cash.'

They went back on deck. Marçel leaned against the rail and stifled a yawn.

'You should get some sleep Marçel,' Sophie said, stroking his face lovingly. 'You look worn out. You don't have to see Sam until later this afternoon. I can navigate the ship back to Bulahdelah, so that will give you four hours' sleep. How about I wake you at six if you are still asleep?'

'You can come and wake me anytime, darling,' Marçel said, sweeping Sophie up into his arms one more time before descending down into the cabin.

CHAPTER 12

'Two down and one to go, Sam.' Marçel leaned forward and helped Sam adjust his pillows. Sam had insisted he be taken to the small but excellent hospital at Bulahdelah where he was able keep his finger on the pulse of the situation without arousing the attention of the media, until the case was finalised and the gold returned to the Australian government

Marcel sat back in his chair grinning. 'I will never forget the look on Kenny's face when your men arrived on the scene; he ran to the door, fully expecting to see that Paul had come back for him.'

'He is an evil man but evil bullies are also cowards at heart; I bet there are quite a few people around the world who would be pleased to know Kenny is now safely locked up.'

'So now we have both of them, and we now know what brought them to Australia, but we have yet to catch the criminal who organised the whole enterprise,' said Marçel. Sam smiled weakly; he was still in considerable pain.

'All that gold!' Marçel continued excitedly. 'It really is amazing. But now there are so many more questions: who does the gold belong to? Where did it come from? How did the criminals find out about it? Moreover, who has been the mastermind behind all of this? Who is trying to steal the gold?'

'It's like a Treasure Island story, complete with pirates

and a mystery Long John Silver with his pirate ship,' Sophie remarked.

'As soon as I get out of this place, I will get back to the station and interrogate Paul and Kenny. I have asked the chief if they can wait until I get there. It's so frustrating lying here when there is so much to do.'

'We understand, Sam. Is there anything that Marcel and I can do for you while we wait?' Sophie held his hand.

'Not really Sophie. But stick around because I'll need your help when I'm back on my feet. We need to track down Charles and maybe find the mastermind behind these killings.'

'The Pirate King,' Sophie interjected.

Sam laughed and continued: 'Paul actually thought that he had made a smart move. Had he waited for the ferry and taken the other route, he would most likely have gotten away. And do you know what? We found one gold nugget on him; he even had to rob his employers! That's certainly not honesty amongst thieves.' Sam gave a grunt as he pulled himself higher up the pillows.

'It would not have been too difficult for a man of his ability, and connections, not to mention the gold and to slip out of Australia. Airport security is good, but with a stolen passport and a complete change of appearance, he might have managed to escape. Stowing away on a ship would have been far less risky. A private aircraft, even if it had the range to reach Indonesia, would be followed on radar and would be intercepted and arrested on reaching its destination.' He turned to Sophie.

'I think you will be safe now, Sophie. I don't think Charles can harm you now that he has lost his two assassinators.'

'I think you are right, Sam, but I shan't feel safe until

Charles is behind bars.' She moved her hand up to his shoulder. 'I am so relieved that your wound is not serious, Sam. I'm sure it will heal up soon. Do you have any family – someone you'd like us to call?'

Sam laughed. 'Why do you want to know? Do you fancy me?' He grinned, reached out and took Sophie's hand. 'No. I'm single Sophie. My rellies all live in Melbourne, but if you were not already in love with this man beside me, I would certainly be chasing after you.'

Marçel stood up and stretched himself. 'You had better watch your step, Sammy boy; or you might find yourself in here for a much longer time.' Marçel chuckled and then returned to the subject.

'So far, we know that Charles came to Australia on a scheduled flight, Sam. We don't actually know how Paul and Kenny got into Australia.'

Sophie went and stared out of the window. 'We know they came in by sea and landed on the beach at a quiet spot where they were able to unload all the equipment, and then transport it to where we found it in the bunker.' She turned to face Sam and Marçel.

'There are a lot of unanswered questions, Sophie. It is possible that they landed at Broughton Island and then ferried everything across to a quiet spot on the ocean beach close to the camping site,' Sam mused.

'Paul and Kenny are just the hired hands. There must be a big-time criminal involved in this enterprise and he must have invested a lot of money into the effort. But the question is – how on earth did they know about the bunker, Sam?' Sophie went and sat on the bed again.

'Apparently no one in all of Australia had any idea of its existence. We've been told that there are no records of this bunker in Canberra. Yet it had a concrete front with a steel door and was full of World War Two arms and ammunition and all that gold.' Marcel sighed. 'We certainly need to have a quiet talk with our prisoners.'

He added, 'We could take Kenny back to the cave and threaten to lock him in if he doesn't speak. I'm sure that would loosen his tongue.'

'This is Australia, Marçel, not the British Army in Afghanistan. I can understand the secret arms caches being established, in case of invasion by the Japanese so that they would be available for some sort of resistance later. I suppose the reason was to keep it secret so that no records could ever fall into the hands of an occupying force. But that gold; why on earth would the war office take it there?' Sam leaned back on his pillows.

'Perhaps they had arranged for someone to collect it and take it out of the country?' Marçel noticed the tired look on Sam's face.

'Well yes, and someone nearly did but thanks to both you and Sophie the gold will remain in Australia.' Sam closed his eyes.

'It seems to me that the money was intended to be moved by someone and maybe it was to be used to fund resistance operations in Australia and most likely other countries in South Asia. I think something very bad must have happened to the people who built the bunker and deposited the arms and gold there. And looking at the ammunition cases, I'd say they were definitely Australian or British, and not American,' Sam mumbled.

Marçel decided to let him rest until morning.

'Sophie and I will stop and have one or two beers at the pub on our way back to the boat, Sam. There might be some old local who remembers something about the goings-on in the area during the war.'

'Have one for me, Marçel. I intend to join you at the pub tomorrow. I owe you one or three. There is one old bloke there they call Clam; he has very long whiskers and he has always lived in the district. Try having a word with him, though you might have to get him a bit tipsy first.'

Sophie stood up and yawned. 'I think you should go alone, Marçel. I have a feeling that if I'm there, the old man will be less likely to speak to you. I'll see you back at the boat.'

★

The main bar was surprisingly quiet. Marçel spotted the old man sitting in a corner holding an almost empty schooner in his hand.

Marçel asked the barman which beer the old man drank, and ordered another two schooners of the same brew. He then crossed over to him, carrying a glass in each hand. 'Have one on me, Dad,' he grinned.

The old man emptied his glass and with a toothless smile took the schooner from Marçel. He wriggled over to one side of the bench. 'It's Great-Granddad to you, boy. Plonk your arse here and tell me why ya stand an old bugger like me a beer. Yer muss want somfing.'

'Well Great-Granddad, it wasn't just your ugly face. Yes, I wanted to ask you a few questions about the lakes and what it was like here during the Second World War. Have you always lived in Bulahdelah and were you actually living here at that time?'

'You're a cheeky kid, aren't yer? Yes, no, yes. Always bin here; fought in first war; fished the lakes ter feed the Yanks in second war. Made good money then!'

He handed Marçel his empty glass. 'Thirsty work all this chat, aye?'

Taking the fresh schooner with well-practised shaking hands, he took a long drink without spilling a single drop. 'Yo can call me Clam, 'cause I'se know how to keep me gob shut. Made a lot of mess around the lakes them Yanks. Dug holes, then filled them up all over the place. But they liked our fish, mullet and black fish, bream and sometimes river bass. They was good times.'

Clam wiped his eyes with a grubby sleeve. 'Till they buggered up my mate, Moley. One day they caught him where he was not meant to be; having a sticky beak he was, nosing in their field office.'

Clam took a long, thoughtful swig on his beer.

'Beat his brains out, they did. He never spoke a word after that.' Clam then clammed up. Marçel, intrigued by this story, wondered what it was that this Moley chap had seen.

'That's all I'se tellin' yer, kid. I never tell anyone this; they only laugh and show disrespect for me mate, Moley.'

'I'm with the British Army, Clam, and would really like you to tell me the entire story. I might be able to help you find out why they did that to Moley.'

Clam's eyes narrowed. He smiled slightly. 'I like you, kiddo. So what's this story worth to yer?' He realised this meeting with the young soldier was not a chance meeting. This young army bloke was looking for information, which only he had knowledge of.

Marçel took out a $100.00 note from his wallet and laughingly waved it at Clam who pulled a face partly concealed by his whiskered face.

'That's an insult to me mate, Holey Moley. Piss off kiddo – your highness. Moley was a fine cultured young man like you, an 'e should have been in the army in them days; said he was a conshee objector or somefing.'

Marçel added another four hundreds and waved them under Clam's nose. 'A lot of schooners there, Clam. Your secret will be safe with me.'

Clam grabbed the notes and stuffed them in his pocket. 'Wot I tells yer stays in yer head and I will deny ever having said a fing to yer.'

Marçel took Clam's horny old hand and shook it vigorously.

"E'd bin gone a few days, when one evening, when I'd bin fishin' a way past the Yanks' camp, he suddenly came running down through the trees. It was a mangrove part there. I pulled to the edge of the mangrove and covered in mud, he scrambled onto the boat. He waved for me to cross over to the other side of the lake. I could see he ad blood all over 'im and it was cummin' from 'is mouth.' Clam gave a shudder and drank from his half-empty glass.

'He said nuffin'. I could see he had been beaten an' he mus' 'ave lost 'is tongue. When we got to the other side, he pointed to me and then to 'imself, then touched 'is lips. I knew wot 'e meant. He hugged me; embarrassed I was, He pointed at the Yanks the other side, made a slit frote sign an' pointed at 'imself. Then he shook me 'ands, jumped out of the boat, ran to the trees and that was the last I ever saw of 'im.'

Marçel went over to the bar and came back with two full glasses.

'You mean you never saw or heard anything about him after that?'

'I swore not to tell, didn't I?' He knocked back half his glass of beer. 'There was talk here in the bar for a time but they thought 'e 'ad gone back to Sydney.'

Marçel realised he would not get much from Clam now; his eyes had a vacant look and his head started to droop. Then he shook himself. 'Funny thing, years after, in the '70s and '80s, people reported seeing a whiskered old man running through the trees at one of the loneliest parts of the lake but no one ever got near to him or found a camp where he lived.'

'That's remarkable, Clam. He could still be alive.'

'Nah, he's long gone. Folks 'as seen 'is ghost. He's long gone an' that's why we calls 'im Holey Moley.' Clam's eyes closed and he gave sleepy grunt.

The barman came over, put his arms around Clam gently lifting him, and guided him to the door. 'Your granddaughter is here to fetch you, Clam. We'll see you in the morning,' he chuckled, 'like every other morning.'

Marçel said good night and wandered down to the cruiser, his mind racing. What Clam had told him might well be connected to this case. The man that he had heard running through the wet bushland and his dying scream when he was murdered, could possibly have been Holey Moley.

It occurred to Marçel that perhaps Holy Moley was the key to solving the mystery as to how the criminals had discovered the bunker hidden inside the cave.

Perhaps Moley knew all about the cave and had been somehow forced to disclose its whereabouts.

Marçel's thoughts were interrupted by the delicious smell of cooking coming from the cruiser. He leaped on board and was greeted with a glass of champagne and a long gentle kiss resulting in a lot of wasted champers. The slight smell of burning abruptly ended the kiss, as both his and Sophie's minds turned to the thought of food.

CHAPTER 13

'Good afternoon, Charles.'

Charles woke up to a sharp pain in his left hand. He looked down to see the stub of a cigarette that had left a searing burn in his skin just by the top of his thumb. He shook it off and then looked up to see Karl in swimming shorts, towering over him.

Charles, lying in one of the poolside recliners, began to sweat. He'd eaten a grilled barramundi for lunch and changed into his swimmers in an attempt to relax. It wasn't the heat of the day that was causing Charles to sweat; he glanced down at the black mark on the back of his hand. It was extremely painful, but nothing next to the fear that Karl's appearance had instilled in him.

'There was no need to do that, Karl,' he whined.

Karl gave a hollow laugh. 'That is nothing compared with what is coming to you, you turd. Take me up to your room; I'm sure the hall porter is used to seeing you taking men up there.' He snapped, 'Now!'

Charles leaped up from the recliner, stubbing his toe on the side table in his rush to obey.

'Now let's have a happy look of anticipation on your face, Charles dear. I'm right behind you; holding a knife inside my bath-robe,' Karl hissed.

'Everything all right, sir?' To Charles's surprise, the young Indian porter addressed Karl; it was the same young man that had come to him last night. Charles suddenly realised this young man had been paid by Karl to keep an eye on him. 'You bastard,' he murmured

'Let me know if you need anything tonight, sir,' the porter called as they entered the lift.

Charles stopped outside his door; Karl pushed him over to the next door, unlocked it and pulled Charles into the room. Karl punched Charles on the nose at the same time he brought his knee up viciously striking Charles in the groin; Charles collapsed on the floor writhing in agony and with blood spurting from his nose. 'Stop it Karl. What have I done?' He screamed.

Karl grabbed Charles' arm and heaved him on to the bed. 'Read this!' He shoved the morning newspaper into Charles' hands.

Charles looked down at the front page headlines and read the first two lines.

TWO MEN ARRESTED ON THE LAKES
IN CONNECTION WITH GIRL'S MURDER

★

'Oh my God …' He was lost for words.

'You've messed up, Charles.' Karl grabbed Charles by the neck. You had better tell me all about it. Don't you remember what I promised if you three failed in this mission?'

Charles knew he was now very close to death and the promise Karl had made was that it would be slow and very painful. His mind raced.

He had only one chance left. At best, this might give him a quick and less painful way out.

'Well, Turd?' Karl released his grip on Charles. 'Talk.'

'It all started when I realised I was being followed by that girl,' Charles whined. 'I was on my way to meet up with the other two men.'

'Was that the same woman who looked into our meeting in London? You told me she was not a problem. Looks like you were wrong.' He was unable to resist striking Charles again, several times across the face.

'Go on, Turd. Let's hear the rest of this disastrous business.'

In between his sobs, a mixture of pain and fear, Charles poured out the whole story including the part about the girl's hand.

Karl sat in the chair opposite Charles, his expression black as thunder. Eventually he spoke. 'You stupid incompetent fools! Not only have you screwed up the whole mission, not only have you wasted all the money we have put into this enterprise, but you have lost us all millions of dollars' worth of gold. I, myself, will be in deep trouble over this failure.'

He got up and stood over the cringing Charles.

'I promised you three that if you failed me in this, you would die a nasty slow death. I will keep this promise. You will be the first, Charles, and I will arrange the slow deaths of the other two when they start their jail sentences.'

Charles in desperation decided to play his last card. At least Karl might reward him with a quick death.

'It's not all lost, Karl. Before the other men arrived, I took the precaution of removing some of the gold to another place.'

'You lying, thieving little runt. You mean you stole gold from me?' he thundered.

'No, Karl! I put it in a safe place just in case anything happened before we were able to complete the transfer of the gold to the beach,' Charles wheezed. 'I'll take you there if you spare my life.' He stupidly added, 'And perhaps I could have some of that gold.'

Karl laughed.

'Oh really. That's very kind of you Charles. We'd better put some clothes on then, and you can show me where it is.'

Karl slipped on some jeans and a sweatshirt and guided Charles back into his own room.

Charles shakily dressed in shorts and T-shirt.

'Do I need a jacket, Karl?' he asked, his voice still trembling.

Karl smiled. 'Not where you're going,' he mumbled.

'The police will have found the launch, Charles, but you still have the truck and trailer. We will need to get another inflatable with a good outboard motor as we will be taking the remainder of the gold out to Broughton Island tonight.'

'That's no problem. We can pick up a good second-hand one at Raymond Terrace on our way through.' Charles picked up his wallet and tried to surreptitiously slip his mobile phone into his pocket. 'I will still have plenty of your money left.'

'That's good, Charles; you won't need much after that. But use your mobile, which you just tried to conceal, to phone the boat yard.' Karl smiled. He decided that Charles wouldn't need much of anything after today.

Charles called a boatyard at Raymond Terrace and was told an almost new, medium-sized inflatable, with a powerful outboard would be ready for him by late afternoon.

It was almost dark when they arrived at a deserted camping site with the inflatable; as a precaution, they chose a different camping site, but near to the one they had used previously. They also bought some food on their way through Raymond Terrace.

They waited until 4.00 am before launching the inflatable into the lake. Charles took the helm and they sped across the lake to the small inlet, close to the cave and bunker. He stopped a short distance from the inlet, by which time there was just enough light to see the outline of the trees overhanging the lake.

'Do you see there are two large swamp mahogany trees standing next to each other, and now there are two more trees on the other side of the inlet that are in line?' Charles asked Karl, trying to relocate the exact spot of the gold from his memory. 'Right now, we are exactly where the two lines cross, which mean the gold bars are right under us. This water is shallow enough to stand in.'

'Then just jump in and pass the gold bars to me, Charles.' Karl growled. 'If you are lying, then you'll be staying down there for good.'

At that moment, a powerful light shone down from the hillside bunker. The two men were startled.

'Seems the police were expecting us to return, Charles,' Karl murmured.

'Perhaps the gold is still there? If it's only one policeman – perhaps we could overpower him and collect all the gold.'

'Don't be so stupid, Charles. We have got to get out of here fast. There is another policeman running down and he is holding a mobile phone as well as a gun.'

'On second thoughts, it seems we are just out of range from their guns,' Karl said. 'Stay in the boat. I'll be much quicker than you.' He dived into the water and came up clutching a gold bar, which he passed over the side of the boat to Charles. He ducked back down and pulled up another, then another, until he had passed all the bars to Charles.

'That's the lot, Karl,' Charles said nervously, looking at the two policemen who were now wading out towards them and realising they would soon be in range of their guns.

'I think we had better get out of here now.' Karl jumped back in the boat and started the motor. The inflatable roared back out onto the lake.

Just as it started to pick up speed, Charles leaped overboard and started furiously swimming towards the nearby mud bank.

Karl was left with two choices, turn back and kill Charles or just get the hell out of there. He took out his gun and fired at what he thought might be Charles; a volley of shots came back from the lakeside bank. Not knowing whether he had hit Charles or not, he decided it was time to cut and run. Anyway, perhaps the police bullets might kill Charles and save him the job. At least he had the gold.

Charles received a bullet in his right leg from Karl, but watched with relief as the inflatable suddenly turned and sped away. He managed to swim towards the men on the shore and was relieved when the police officers, who were guarding the bunker, promptly arrested him.

★

The sky was just beginning to lighten, so Karl had no difficulty in finding the right camping site with the truck and trailer.

He pulled the inflatable up onto the ramp and ran across to the parking area to bring the truck and trailer over to the boat. As he loaded the inflatable, he noticed several new campers walking towards him. Karl took out his revolver and fired a few shots in their direction; they immediately scattered and ran back to their newly erected tents.

Karl drove out onto the main road and just a few yards later, turned off onto a track that ran down to the ocean beach.

He drove along the beach for a short distance and then

backed the trailer down to the water's edge, launching the inflatable, abandoning the truck and trailer. Karl started the motor and headed out into the surf. Luckily he was able to dodge the breaking waves and was soon heading out to sea towards Broughton Island.

He used his two-way radio to call his radio operator who was waiting on Broughton Island. Karl instructed him to contact the submarine to tell them that they were on their way back to the submarine. A few minutes later when he reached Broughton Island's sheltered beach, he picked up the wireless operator, who gave him the submarine's exact position, and they headed straight out to sea.

The sky was clearing into day as they headed towards the rising sun. The other man took the tiller while Karl got down on to his knees and prayed.

The sea was relatively calm so they made good progress. The land behind them was almost out of sight when they spotted the submarine dead ahead of them. His colleague had done his job well.

They came alongside the sheltered side of the submarine and clambered aboard.

It was at that moment that Karl heard the distant rumble of jets.

They scrambled down into the submarine followed by the crew members; the hatch closed behind them for the last time.

CHAPTER 14

Marçel woke to the incessant ringing of his mobile phone. Sophie put her arm out to feel that he was still there. He bent over and kissed her before answering the call.

'Who's calling me in the middle of the night?' He guessed it must be Geoff. It was.

'Sorry to wake the young lovers. Don't worry, I know all about your love life, but don't be alarmed, it's part of the job,' he laughed.

'Where the hell are you, Geoff?'

'I am in a helicopter and about to touch down on a grass strip near your river bridge. It's on the opposite side of the river to where you are moored. Come and meet me.'

Marçel returned to the cabin. 'We have a visitor, Sophie. He's in a chopper and it's just landed on the other side of the bridge.'

'Wow, who would want to come here in the middle of the night, in a chopper?'

'My boss.' Marçel slipped on some trousers and a windcheater. 'Better put the kettle on, darling. I think we will all need a cup of tea when he gets here.'

Marçel decided to take his Land Rover, in case Geoff had any luggage. The helicopter had already landed when he arrived at the small park next to the bridge. Geoff ducked his head and ran over to Marçel. They embraced, pleased to see each other again.

The pilot switched off the motor and waited for the rotor

to stop. He locked up and joined them, carrying two large bags.

'Marçel, this is Wayne. He's a top-notch chopper pilot. Brought us here at very short notice and came straight to this place; no problem.'

'Good to meet you, Wayne. That's something I would love to do, fly a helicopter.' Wayne shook his hand.

'It's not very hard. If we have time in the morning, I will give you a spin and you can have a feel of the controls.'

'Let's get over to your cruiser, Marçel; I hope there's room for another two people.' Geoff had little time for idle chatter. He needed to talk to Marçel as soon as possible.

'No problem, there is plenty of room and the kettle should be boiling by now. I have a wonderful girlfriend called Sophie.'

'Yes Marçel. I know all about young Sophie. You are very lucky. She is a very brave young lady.'

Sophie was holding tea bags in her hand as she beckoned the visitors to step aboard the cruiser. 'Welcome on board! I'm pleased to finally meet Marçel's boss, and pilot. Tea is almost ready.'

Geoff put his arms around Sophie, gently kissing her on both cheeks.

'Marçel is certainly lucky to have a friend like you. But I think he will need a little domestic training. Lucky boy!' Geoff laughed.

'Please don't frighten the poor boy off. I have had to work hard in capturing him,' Sophie answered in fun, but in her mind was a little worried that their romance might be moving too fast and because of that, it might not last. That she could not bear.

★

'So what brings you here in the middle of the night in a helicopter, Geoff?' Marçel asked and then added with enthusiasm, 'This case is going quite well. We now have two of the killers, but it's a pity that Detective Sam Morrow got injured.'

'Marçel, I'm afraid there is a much more serious aspect to this business. What I am about to tell you is top secret and must not go outside these walls. I mean this cruiser. That includes you, Sophie; that is if you want to go along with us? If you do, you will have to sign this piece of paper; a section of the Secrecy Act. This will bind you to it for the rest of your life. Wayne and Marçel are already sworn in.'

'I want to see this through, Geoff.' Sophie took the form, read it and signed the bottom line. Geoff then added his signature to the document.

'Now let me begin.' Geoff's tone of voice had changed. He was now the senior officer briefing his team.

'We have been closely following the activities of the man who is behind the recovery of all this gold and which you have now brought to light.' Geoff paused to let this sink in.

'He uses the name of Karl Grunsteig and is a well-known international criminal. However, we do know his real identity and that he comes from Russia. He's one of the top terrorists in the world. I am sorry I cannot give you any more details. He is a very dangerous man and we do not want the world to know that we are about to eliminate him. You can imagine the repercussions.' He paused to let this sink in.

'The reason I have just come from Canberra is that we have just finalised a plan to secretly eliminate this man. Now you will understand all this secrecy. I am waiting for a call which should come any minute now.'

'Can you really do this? Why not just arrest this man?' Sophie was a little shocked by Geoff's matter-of-fact tone.

'The recovery of the gold is the last piece to fit into this horrific jigsaw. It was meant to be used as the final payment for a large number of Dirty Atom Bombs. Believe me; the whole damn world is in danger.' There was a deadly silence around the table.

Geoff's phone broke the silence.

'Yes …Yes. Right … Yes, we are ready; we'll wait for your call. That's great news. Congratulate your boys.' Geoff put his phone on the table.

'I have some good news for you, Sophie. Your man Charles has been taken prisoner. Apparently he stashed away some of the gold, which he and Karl went to recover. Our lads, who had been left to guard the bunker, spotted them and called us. To our chaps' surprise, we told them to wait and let them get away. They set off into the lake but then Charles bailed out of the inflatable; Charles was swimming in the lake when Karl shot him in the leg but he just kept going. Charles swam to the shore and was promptly arrested.'

'Why did you let Karl go?' Marçel asked.

'It's all part of the plan; we're about to set off in the helicopter to watch the final episode of this dreadful business.'

'I suggest you guys put on something warm to wear. It can get quite nippy up there,' Wayne advised them. Marçel could see he was impatient to get going.

Fifteen minutes later, Wayne got a call from his base at Newcastle.

'All set to go, sir. The inflatable has left Broughton Island and is heading due east and out to sea.'

Geoff sat next to Wayne while Marçel and Sophie sat behind. They all had a clear vision; they put on their headsets and the chopper took off.

It was now almost daylight, and the chopper skimmed across the lake, over the large sand hills that over the years, were slowly moving inland, the wind-driven sand slowly devouring all the vegetation in its path as it gradually moved towards the Myall Lake.

Then they skimmed across the sea to Broughton Island, unoccupied except for the occasional camping fishermen. They continued in an easterly direction. 'We should see their inflatable any time now. I don't want to get ahead of them, so keep an eye out for them.' Wayne took the chopper up to two thousand feet.

'I can see something ahead; it's slightly on our left,' Sophie yelled.

'That's it! The submarine can't be too far away. Best drop back a little now, Wayne. We don't want to alert them. Although I'm sure a helicopter will not worry Karl, now that he is so near to home.' Geoff was searching the sky.

'I can see the submarine now, Geoff,' Wayne said calmly.

'Right. You two in the back are about to see an execution. You will never speak of this event to anyone now or in the future. Understand?'

'Yes, boss. Our mouths and eyes are sealed.'

'The inflatable has come alongside the submarine.' Geoff's voice rose slightly. 'Now look up to your right-hand side.'

They watched as three jet fighter-bombers, in line ahead, dived down towards the surfaced submarine. The roar of the jets as they passed in front the helicopter drowned out the sounds of the explosion that split the submarine in two.

They watched as the two halves disappeared under the dark blue ocean.

The four remained silent for a few moments. They had witnessed the deaths of an unknown number of men.

'That was a bit drastic, Geoff. There might have been a lot of innocent men on that boat.' Sophie was shocked at the violence of what she had just seen.

'My dear, if they were innocent people they would not have been on that submarine.' Geoff reached over and held Sophie's hand. 'If we had not stopped these people and they had taken delivery of their dirty bombs, perhaps millions of innocent people might have died.'

Another helicopter flew past them, the sun reflecting on the gold-braided uniforms of the senior staff officers from Canberra.

Both helicopters circled slowly around the area where the submarine had been destroyed, until it was obvious that there were no survivors.

Wayne flew them back to Bulahdelah. Sophie and Marçel got out of the chopper and Geoff followed.

Sophie took Geoff's arm. 'Just one question Geoff, if there had been survivors what would you have done with them?'

Geoff put his arms around Sophie, hugged her, and kissed her on both cheeks. 'We had not planned to have any survivors, Sophie; I think you understand that.'

'Yes you are right; I do realise it was just not possible.' She kissed him lightly on the cheek. 'Your job is to keep the world safe, no matter the cost. Thank you.'

'I hope I am going to see a lot more of you in the future, Sophie.' Geoff shook hands with Marçel. 'You did a good job there, Marçel, but I expect to see you back in your London office in three weeks' time. So go and get yourself a ticket to London today. And Sophie, you had better go back with him or else you will find you have lost your job! See you both in London.'

★

Geoff got back in the chopper and in just a few seconds they were climbing out over the slow-moving Myall River.

They returned to the cruiser to find Sam sitting on the deck having made himself a cup of coffee.

'There is plenty more in the galley, guys,' he grinned.

'Thanks, Sam. Don't get up.' Marçel grinned.

'Can't anyway. Unless Sophie helps me,' he laughed.

'I intend to get back on the job tomorrow. I have a lot of questions to ask those three men we have under arrest, and I think that will only be the start of things. A number of locals who were around here during the war will have to be interviewed. A lot of old records in Canberra will have to be examined, and so on. Should be interesting,' Sam mused.

'I wouldn't count on it,' Marçel said. I think Canberra has cleaned up with all this recovered gold; they will clam up on this event and will now want to put all this behind them. It might reveal too many skeletons in the war office cupboards.'

Sam nodded, and he almost looked disappointed.

'Look Sam, I've paid for this cruiser for another two weeks. Why don't you stay here, make it your base for the next two weeks and try and relax until you get your strength back.'

'That's a great offer, Marçel. I think I'll have to take you up on that. It's just what the doctor ordered. But when am I going to see you two again?'

'Next Christmas; we're coming back for a holiday here

on the lakes for a few weeks and I hope you will be able to come and stay with us in London next year,' Sophie said.

'Will we be hearing the sound of wedding bells?'

'Maybe Sam, but I will need a best man if we do,' Marçel grinned.

Sophie looked surprised, and her face reddened a little. 'I really don't know what to say. He hasn't asked me yet, but I hope he will.'

She wondered why Sam was suddenly grinning; she looked down to see Marcel kneeling at her feet.

'Have you lost something, Marcel?' she giggled.

'For heaven's sake get on with it Marcel, or else I will,' Sam laughed.

Marcel stood up and took Sophie's hands in his. 'Sophie, will you do me the honour of becoming my wife, till death do us part?'

'Oh, my God,' Sam murmured.

'Yes – yes – YES …'

Sophie flung her arms around Marcel and they kissed whilst the world stood still.

Sam looked at his watch, commenting: 'Ten minutes and still going!'

ALSO BY
Richard Le Normand...

1943—the German-occupied island of Jersey.

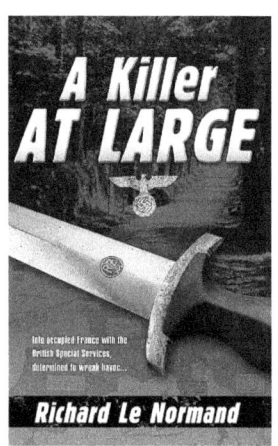

A sixteen-year old boy is brutally raped by German soldiers and deported to France where he escapes, and becomes obsessed with revenge.

After joining the French Resistance and proving his worth, he is chosen for a covert British Special Services 'operation'.

A non-stop, no frills, action-packed roller coaster of a thriller, thoroughly researched and written by master story teller Richard Le Normand, a Jerseyman who lived through the Occupation and who is now retired and lives on the Gold Coast in Queensland, Australia.

ALSO BY
Richard Le Normand...

I n 1947 Marcel, Peter and Gerda, working for a special branch of the secret service, run an escape route from Germany, through France and Spain, to their castle on the Portuguese coast. The clients are minor war criminals; each one carries a case of gold, stolen from their concentration camp victims.

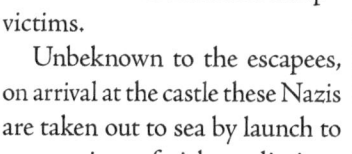
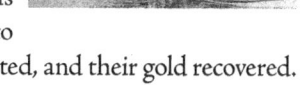

Unbeknown to the escapees, on arrival at the castle these Nazis are taken out to sea by launch to a non-existent freighter, eliminated, and their gold recovered. This is their 'escape to death' …

Karl, a distant relative and protégé of Adolph Hitler, hopes to revive the Nazi party and become the second führer of Germany. He arrives in Portugal from South America to find out what has happened to his colleagues and the gold.

Marçel, Helga and Gerda, having survived the motor accident that killed all the clients, arrive at the castle to find total carnage. Stephen, Marçel's boss, arrives from London to help, and to cover-up the operation.

So begins a cat and mouse game in which Karl tries to kidnap the girls and recover the gold. Mick, an Australian survivor of the Spanish civil war, becomes involved with his ketch and a classic battle between good and evil is played out on land and sea.